———————— ★ ————————

I peeked into the car. Oh, God. There was something in the front seat. Not something. Someone. Maybe the person was drunk, sleeping it off because he'd heeded the warning not to drink and drive.

My own heart was in my throat. My breath was coming in raspy gasps because of the blockage to my air passage.

I tapped on the window. No response. I did it again. Still nothing. I went over to the passenger-side door, but I stopped before I grabbed the handle. Be smart. I took a Kleenex out of my purse and used it to hold on to the handle. I yanked on the door.

The person's head, which had been wedged up against the armrest, fell forward toward me. It was Frank Pankovich.

———————— ★ ————————

"Dolores Johnson is an author to watch, and Mandy Dyer is a character to laugh with."

—*I Love a Mystery*

Dolores Johnson

BUTTONS & FOES

W❂RLDWIDE.

TORONTO • NEW YORK • LONDON
AMSTERDAM • PARIS • SYDNEY • HAMBURG
STOCKHOLM • ATHENS • TOKYO • MILAN
MADRID • WARSAW • BUDAPEST • AUCKLAND

To my sisters-in-law, Mildred Johnson
and Elaine Jackson

BUTTONS & FOES

A Worldwide Mystery/March 2004

First published by St. Martin's Press LLC.

ISBN 0-373-26487-9

Printed in U.S.A.

Acknowledgments

I wish to thank Barbara Reiter, cochairperson of the 2001 National Button Society Meeting and Show in Denver, and Hal Snyder of the Prairie Pedlar and Armchair Auctions in Lyons, Kansas, for answering my questions on button collecting. I also found helpful information in *About Buttons* by Peggy Ann Osborne, *Buttons* by Nancy Fink and Maryalice Ditzler, *Buttons* by Diana Epstein, and "Button Collecting, A Lifetime Voyage of Discovery" by M. W. Speights in *Antiques and Art Around Florida*. In addition, I wish to thank Detective Gary Hoffman of the Denver Police Department for answering my questions on police procedures. Any errors in this book are mine and not the fault of the people mentioned above.

As always, I owe a debt of gratitude to members of my two critique groups—Rebecca Bates, Thora Chinnery, Diane Coffelt, Cindy Goff, Donna Schaper, and Barbara Snook; and to Lee Karr, Kay Bergstrom, Carol Caverly, Diane Davidson, Christine Jorgensen, Leslie O'Kane, and Peggy Swager.

Finally, special thanks to my agents, Meg Ruley and Ruth Kagle, and to my editor, Marcia Markland.

ONE

THE WOMAN WASN'T a typical dry-cleaning customer. She looked like Elvira-turned-Biker Babe. Or maybe Morticia Addams as a bag lady since she was dragging two huge trash bags as she came into Dyer's Cleaners.

"I'm looking for the owner—someone named Mandy Dyer," she said.

"I'm Mandy," I said. "What can I do for you?"

The Biker Babe could have been anywhere from her early twenties to late thirties. Her heavy makeup and almost-black lipstick made it hard to tell. Her long dark hair—unlike mine, which is short and brown—seemed to have been sprayed on with jet-black ink. She was wearing tight black leather pants, jacket, and boots. The only thing missing was a Harley, but of course, she couldn't have hauled the trash bags on a motorcycle.

She hoisted the bags onto the counter and gave me a bored look. "I'm helping out my boyfriend, and he wanted me to bring you these old clothes."

I looked inside one of the bags, where I could see a couple of wadded-up and faded cotton dresses, one in plaid and the other in a floral pattern. "Did he want them laundered and pressed?" The dresses certainly weren't the type that customers brought us to be cleaned.

"You kiddin'?" She snorted and shrugged the shoulders of her motorcycle jacket. "His great-aunt wanted you to have 'em."

I tried again. "And what did she want me to do with them?"

"Beats me. She said you'd know."

Unfortunately, I didn't. I dug down into one of the bags, but all I saw were more housedresses and cotton-blend housecoats, all as worn as the ones on top. "I wonder if she intended them for our clothing drive?" I asked.

This was a Monday in early October, and we'd be putting out our collection box within the next few weeks for the drive that culminated just before Christmas. Mainly, we wanted children's clothing and heavy coats for Denver's cold winters, but I supposed we could always use the dresses—the ones that weren't completely worn out—for residents at the battered women's shelters.

Biker Babe shrugged again.

"I'll hold on to them," I said, starting to remove the bags from the counter, "but why don't you ask your boyfriend's aunt if that's what she had in mind before we give them away?"

"I can't ask her," the woman said. "She's dead."

That stopped me, and I put the bags back on the counter. "Who was she?"

"Thelma Chadwick, but Deke hadn't seen her since he was a kid."

I gave a little gasp at the mention of the name. Thelma had been one of my favorite customers, an elderly woman who'd always had a great curiosity and enthusiasm for life. Even though she'd assured me she was feeling okay the last time I'd seen her, I'd assumed she died of natural causes when I read about her death in the obituaries two weeks ago.

"I was really sorry to hear of her death," I said. "Please give my condolences to Deke. I gather he's the nephew."

"Yeah, but like I said, he didn't even know her."

There was something wrong here. "But you said Thelma told him to give me the clothes."

"Oh, yeah, I guess I forgot to mention that. His aunt wrote it down and attached it to her will"—Biker Babe snorted—"like she had anything worth leaving in a will."

I was hung up on that first thing the woman had said. Why would Thelma leave me these bags of old clothing in a handwritten codicil to her will?

And besides that, Biker Babe's indifferent attitude toward Thelma upset me. When I saw Thelma's obituary, I sent a sympathy note in care of her address. I'd hoped her family would receive it, but I wasn't sure a guy with a girlfriend like this was the type of relative I would have wished for her.

"I hope she wasn't ill for long," I said, maybe looking for some sign of caring from Biker Babe.

She pulled a pack of cigarettes out of her jacket pocket, then looked around our smoke-free call office, which is what we call the customer area of the plant. She apparently thought better of lighting up. "Oh, she wasn't sick. She had an accident, but her next-door neighbor didn't find the body until the next day."

My heart dropped into the pit of my stomach. I had an image of poor Thelma tripping on one of the throw rugs I'd seen in her knotty-pine living room, breaking her hip, and lying on the floor for hours, unable to get up or reach the phone.

I'd only been in her home one time, just a month before her death. She rented a small white frame house in east Denver, and it looked as if it had been freshly painted when I parked in her driveway that day.

She told me she was going to have to find another place to live because the owner had sold the property. In preparation for the move, she'd asked if I would stop by and get some of her late husband's clothes that she wanted to donate to the clothing drive.

"I would get them myself, but they're down in the basement," she said, "and I can't get down there anymore because of my arthritis."

After I collected the clothes, she invited me into the kitchen for a cup of tea. It was a big, cheerful room with canary-yellow walls.

"It's so dark in the living room with all that woodwork that I spend most of my time out here," she said, motioning to a rocking chair next to the kitchen table. "But to tell the truth, it'll be a relief to move. I had a prowler outside the house a few nights ago."

She went on to say that he was gone by the time the police arrived, but I could tell it still bothered her.

"I don't see why a burglar would try to break in here," she said. "I only have one thing a person might ever want, and it's hidden away where no one can find it."

She looked so worried that I asked her if she was feeling all right.

"Oh, I'm fine," she said. "At least as fine as an old lady like me can be."

Thelma never talked about her illnesses the way

some elderly people do, and despite the increasing ravages of arthritis, she usually had a twinkle in her eyes that made her seem younger than she really was. Maybe I should have guessed her age by her silver-white hair, which she wore in a bun. Still, I'd been surprised when I read in the obituary that she was eighty-six years old.

I'm in my thirties, but the difference in our ages didn't matter. We had a great time discussing our favorite mystery novels, even if our visits were confined to talks over the counter in the cleaners.

Whenever she came by, sometimes without any cleaning to be dropped off or picked up, she always had a couple of paperback books that she wanted me to read. And one of the first things I thought about when I read the obituary was that now I would never be able to return the books she'd loaned me.

Personally, I'd always felt that the reason Thelma liked me was that she was intrigued by my involvement—unintentional, I assure you—in solving several murders. True crime was her real passion, and she loved to read books about such cases.

"I need you to sign something to show you got the clothes," Biker Babe said. "Oh, yeah, and here's a copy of the note. Deke said you wouldn't believe it unless I gave it to you." She pulled it out of a jacket pocket and handed it to me.

I'd been staring into one of the bags of dresses—in disbelief. They didn't look like anything I'd ever seen Thelma wear. She'd favored tailored suits and dresses that were well made and would last forever.

"You get what you pay for," she'd told me once. "Look at this suit, Mandy. I bought it in 1983, and it's still as good as new. If you buy clothes with a classic design, they never go out of style.''

I read the note. It said: ''Give two bags of clothes in hall closet to Mandy Dyer at Dyer's Cleaners. She'll know what to do with them.'' It was exactly what Biker Babe had said.

I realized the woman was moving restlessly from one foot to the other. ''Deke wanted me to get some kind of receipt for the lawyer that you'd received this stuff.''

But my mind was still on Thelma's accident and the strange bags of clothes. ''If you don't mind my asking, what kind of accident did Thelma have?''

''She fell down her basement steps. Landed on her head.''

My heart zoomed up from my chest cavity and into my throat, where I could feel it pounding a warning call. Fortunately, it choked off the words I wanted to scream out about Thelma's death. This woman had to be wrong about where the accident occurred. Thelma couldn't have fallen down the basement stairs. She never went down to the basement. She'd told me so herself.

''If you'll just sign something, I'll get going,'' Biker Babe said impatiently.

''Okay, sure.'' I grabbed a scratch pad we kept on the counter and began to write: ''Received from—''

''What's your name?'' My voice was trembling, but I realized this would be a good way to find out who she was.

She looked over at what I was writing. ''Leilani.'' She spelled it for me. ''Leilani McLaine.'' She spelled that too.

"And what's your boyfriend's name?"

"Dexter Wolfe with an *e* on the end, but you better just put Deke. He hates it when people call him Dexter."

I continued, my handwriting as shaky as my voice: "—as the representative of Deke Wolfe, two bags of clothes."

I reached down into one of the bags. "Do you want a breakdown of how many items are here?"

"Naw." She pinched up her face in disgust. "Just say old clothes, although who the hell would want to wear them, I don't know."

I finished writing and signed my name. "Do you and Deke live here in Denver?"

She shook her head. "No way. We're from L.A., and I can hardly wait till we get the house cleared out so we can head back home. Deke thought his aunt probably had a lot of money, but boy, was he in for a surprise. There wasn't nothing there except a lot of junk like this and some old paperback books." She grabbed the note and started to leave.

"How did you say she died again?"

"Took a header down her basement steps."

My head was still spinning as if I'd just taken a ride in the fifty-pound dryer back in our laundry department, and my mouth felt as parched as if I had.

"I guess the coroner's office investigated her death since no one was with her when she died," I said when I managed to pry my tongue away from the roof of my mouth.

Biker Babe was almost at the door. "Yeah, that's how they knew it was an accident."

"I wonder if they were aware that—"

No, I shouldn't say anything to her about the steps and the horrible thoughts that kept running through my mind. But why hadn't Thelma's next-door neighbor told the police that Thelma never went downstairs?

I tried to remember her house. It faced west toward the mountains, but I didn't know anything about her neighbors. I decided to make up something. "Uh— who found her? Was it that good friend of hers who lived just north of her place?"

Leilani thought about it for a few seconds. "Naw, it was some woman who lived on the other side." She left before I could ask any more questions.

I needed to call someone at the police department and tell them about the stairs and also about the prowler. Unfortunately, the only person I could think to call was Stan Foster, the homicide detective with whom I'd had an on-again, off-again relationship until I'd broken it off in June.

I wasn't sure I wanted to call Stan and open up all those old wounds, but I was positive about one thing. I needed to let someone in a position of authority know that Thelma Chadwick could have been murdered. At the moment, I might be the only person in the world—outside of a killer—who suspected that.

TWO

BEFORE I CALLED the police, I decided I should talk to Mack about my suspicions. He was always the voice of reason when I was about to do something rash.

Mack is a big black man with the voice of James Earl Jones and the build of a retired prizefighter. He'd worked for my late uncle for years, and I'd hoped he'd go into partnership with me when I inherited the cleaners. He preferred to remain plant manager and chief dry cleaner so he would have time to act in amateur theatrical productions around Denver. Too bad I wasn't an employee, too, because then I might have had time to pursue my dream of being an artist instead of spending my time as a glorified rag merchant.

I dragged the two trash bags of clothes past the conveyor of finished garments and the pressing equipment to Mack's station at the dry-cleaning machines. I was almost there when Betty from the laundry department spotted me.

"What's in the bags?" she yelled.

Well, why wouldn't she be interested in Hefty bags? She'd been a real bag lady, after all, and Hefty bags had been her outerwear of choice when she was known, both literally and figuratively, as Betty the Bag

Lady. I was now in the process of trying to rehabilitate her, but there was still a lot of the street person in her.

"Just some old clothes for our clothing drive," I said, trying to shake her off.

"Maybe there'd be something in there that I'd like," she said as I continued walking.

I shook my head. "I don't think so, not unless you're planning to marry Arthur and become a full-time homemaker." Arthur was a chubby doll doctor with a wisp of white hair who'd become enamored with Betty for reasons that were totally unfathomable to me. "They're all housedresses."

I'd never seen Betty in anything but slacks and shirts or an incredibly ugly green polyester pants suit. She had close-cropped gray hair and weathered skin from too much time in the out-of-doors. I'd always thought the deep lines looked like a smile etched into her face from a mysterious but happy past that I knew nothing about. But hard as I tried, I couldn't picture that past as having anything to do with housedresses and domesticity.

"Yuck," Betty said, confirming my view of her.

I continued on to where Mack was putting a load of dark clothes into our big seventy-pound cleaning machine. It was the busy time of day for him and his Korean assistant, Kim, so I knew he couldn't break away right then.

"What's up?" he said as he punched in the program to operate the machine. He returned to the spotting board, where he was in the midst of removing what looked like wine stains from an elaborate royal blue evening gown.

As he continued to work, I spilled out the story of

Thelma and why I had this awful feeling about what had happened to her.

Mack paused with his steam gun poised in the air. "Okay," he said finally, "you said she told you she didn't go down in the basement anymore because of her arthritis, but that doesn't mean a person wouldn't do it under special circumstances."

"But she asked me to go to her house specifically to collect clothes from the basement because she said she couldn't get them."

"Yeah, but maybe that was because she didn't think she could climb the stairs with a whole load of clothes in her arms, not that she couldn't go down there just to look around."

"Maybe." I knew it was good to get another point of view, but somehow I couldn't let go of the idea that Thelma wouldn't have attempted the stairs with her bad knees.

"But we'd also started picking up her laundry whenever she called," I said. "She said her washer and dryer were in the basement and she couldn't get down there to use the machines anymore."

Her house wasn't even on one of our regular pick-up routes, but I'd made an exception in her case. She was one of our longtime customers; she'd even followed Uncle Chet from the downtown plant where he'd started to our present location in what's called the Cherry Creek area of Denver.

"Still, if you were moving, wouldn't you want to go downstairs to see what was there?" Mack asked.

"I suppose," I said, "but listen to this. The nephew's girlfriend told me that Thelma had specifically mentioned in a handwritten note attached to her will that I was to be given these bags of clothes. Isn't that strange?"

"Yeah," Mack conceded, "but maybe it was simply because she was interested in supporting our clothing drive."

"So why didn't she give me the clothes when I was at her house a month before she died?"

"She could have forgotten all about them until she discovered them on one of her trips downstairs, or maybe a friend gave them to her after you were there."

Okay, so everything Mack said sounded logical, but I knew he was trying to diffuse my runaway imagination.

"All right, but there's more." I handed him the note and gave him time to read it. "Thelma says I'll know what to do with the clothes, but I have no idea what she meant. She loved word games—" I stopped as I realized I hadn't told Mack about the prowler. "When I picked up the clothes, Thelma said she'd called the police because there'd been a prowler outside her house. She also said she had something valuable that was hidden away where no one could find it. I wish I'd asked her more about it."

Mack shook his head. "Now, don't go punishing yourself with a lot of what-ifs, Mandy. It doesn't do a bit of good."

That wasn't what I wanted to hear. "Do you suppose the message about my knowing what to do with the clothes could have a double meaning?"

"You mean"—he put down the steam gun—"something like 'Please investigate my death if anything happens to me'?"

I was indignant. "No, more like it was a clue as to where she'd hidden something."

But Mack wasn't going to let me off the hook. "Or maybe she meant exactly what it sounds like—that you'd know the clothes were intended for the clothing drive."

"You think so, huh?" I pulled a blue-and-white-striped dress from the top of the pile inside one of the bags. It had a drooping hem, a ripped seam at the sleeve, and was worn thin from too many washings. "Look at this and tell me she really believed it would be good enough to donate to one of the homeless shelters."

Mack fingered the dress, and even he looked skeptical.

"Maybe I should give Stan a call—"

Mack held up a hand. "You sure you want to do that?"

He knew all about my breakup with the handsome homicide detective and how I'd felt that Stan had left me hanging out to dry, so to speak, when I became a suspect in a homicide investigation during the summer. My much-married mom, now safely back in Phoenix, had been disappointed about the breakup. She'd pointed out that I'd left the door open a crack for a reconciliation when I said we needed time apart to think about our relationship. Stan hadn't tried to reopen that door in the intervening months, and I wasn't sure I wanted to, either.

I looked over at Mack, who seemed to be waiting for an answer. "I don't know anyone else to call," I said.

"Well, go ahead then," Mack said, "since I'm sure you won't leave it alone."

Once I had his seal of approval, more or less, I proceeded to my office, where I hoisted the bags to a sofa at the side of the room and continued to my desk.

Since I'd seldom been able to catch Stan at his desk, I practiced what I'd say to his voice mail. Then I dialed his extension at police headquarters quickly, before I lost my nerve.

To my dismay, he answered his phone.

Now what should I say? "Uh—" Always a good start. "Uh—this is Mandy. How've you been?"

"Mandy? This is a surprise. I've been meaning to call you."

"Oh, really. What about?"

"I—well, I wanted to tell you that I've met someone…"

God, I bet he thought I'd called to tell him I wanted him back. His voice faded away, and I couldn't think of anything to fill the void. I'd gone brain-dead, and I wasn't sure if it was from embarrassment, shock, or jealousy.

"She's a kindergarten teacher," he said finally.

"Good," I said. Maybe she wouldn't go sniffing around in things Stan thought were none of her business, the way he always thought I did. That brought me back to the purpose of my call.

"Look, Stan, I was wondering if you could tell me anything about Thelma Chadwick's death." I paused to take a breath. "She was a good customer of mine, and I know she was alone when she died, so I'm assuming the police looked into her death."

"Oh, damn, Mandy, you're not getting involved in

something again. Haven't you learned your lesson by now?''

"I just wanted to find out the cause of death.''

"You can call the medical examiner's office. Autopsies are public records.''

"But can't you tell me?''

He sighed deeply. "And that will be the end of it?'' I didn't answer, but apparently he took my silence for affirmation. "Hold on a minute. Okay?''

I doodled on a scratch pad while I waited with the phone to my ear.

"You still there?'' he asked after about five minutes.

I said I was.

"Okay, her death was ruled an accident caused by a fall down her basement stairs,'' he said. "There were injuries to her head that were consistent with such a fall.''

"I was just wondering if there was any possibility of foul play. She told me recently that she'd had a problem with a prowler.''

"According to the police report, her doors were locked, and there were no signs of forced entry,'' he said. "Although she appeared to be in the process of moving, the police couldn't find any evidence of a burglary or anything missing from the house.''

"But couldn't she have let someone into the house?'' Someone like a money-hungry nephew, I thought, but I didn't say so.

I realized I'd been drawing what looked like an endless flight of stair steps as I listened to him. "I was concerned because she'd told me that she never went down in the basement anymore because of arthritis.''

"That's not what a neighbor said. She said she saw the light on in Thelma's basement lots of times and was sure Thelma was down there preparing to move."

What could I say to that? Maybe Mack was right and Thelma simply hadn't wanted to risk going up and down the stairs with a big armful of clothes.

Still, I was reluctant to let Stan go. "Uh, how did anyone find her body if her doors were locked?"

"The neighbor hadn't seen her outside that morning, noticed that her drapes were still closed, and went over to check on her. The woman spotted her body through a basement window."

"Who was that—the neighbor, I mean?"

"You know I can't give you that information."

Well, it had been worth a try.

"Let it go, Mandy," Stan said as a parting shot. "It was an accident."

I thanked him for the information and hung up. I probably should have wished him good luck in his new relationship, but I couldn't deal with that right now. Instead I focused on what he'd said about Thelma.

I'd been hoping to get the neighbor's name, but Biker Babe had already told me where she lived. What I needed to do now was drive out to east Denver and talk to her. I would wait until after four o'clock when Mack went home so he wouldn't ask me any questions about where I was going.

For the time being, I went over to the sofa and began pulling dresses out of one of the bags. Each one was as shabby as the one before. No wonder Biker Babe had scoffed about who would want to wear them.

They all looked as if they were candidates for the rag pile.

If they had really belonged to Thelma, she must have worn them in a different life when she'd been a housewife back in World War II. All I knew about her was that she'd never had any children and had been a widow for many years.

I kept pulling out dresses, sure I'd never seen Thelma wear any of them. I was halfway through the bag when I got to a faded green-and-white-striped shirtwaist. Suddenly something unusual caught my eye.

It was the buttons. Mismatched buttons. Dozens of buttons. Down the front and up the sleeves. More buttons than there were buttonholes. I tore through the pile at the bottom of the bag. There were more dresses decorated with unnecessary buttons. Silver buttons. Brass buttons. Big, colorful buttons in abstract designs and geometric patterns. Buttons that looked like flowers and like Mickey Mouse. And shiny bejeweled buttons that could be costume-type imitations or the real thing.

I was practically hyperventilating. Was this what Thelma had wanted me to see—a fortune that her nephew hadn't been able to find?

If a clever old woman who liked to read mysteries wanted to put her wealth into a valuable button collection, what better way to hide it than on a lot of old dresses that no one wanted? And what better place to hide the collection than stuffed at the bottom of a trash bag with a lot of equally worthless garments on top?

I seriously doubted that Biker Babe and her boyfriend had even bothered to go through the bags, and even if they had, would they have thought of the buttons as anything except the silly collection of an eccentric old woman who also collected paperback murder mysteries?

But more importantly, could the buttons have been a motive for murder?

THREE

I GRABBED A RED plaid dress and went looking for Mack again. He wasn't at the cleaning machines, but his assistant, Kim, grinned at me. "Boss man is out to lunch."

Kim works hard to improve his English, and he pronounced each word carefully. The "boss man" was something he'd picked up from Betty, who calls Mack and me "boss man" and "boss lady." I figure it's a lot better than some other things she could have taught him to say.

He pointed in the direction of the break room, and I was relieved that I wouldn't have to wait until Mack returned from a restaurant in the neighborhood.

I hurried back past my office to the break room, where I spotted Mack at a table just beyond the door. The finishing crew wouldn't stop for lunch for half an hour, so I assumed we were alone.

"Look at this." I held up the dress with its dozens of buttons. Unfortunately, it obscured my view of Betty, who was getting a soda out of the pop machine in the corner of the room. "All the dresses at the bottom of the bags have these mismatched buttons on them. I think this is what Thelma meant when she said I'd know what to do with the clothes."

"Well, I'll be damned." Mack glanced from one

kind of button to the next. "So what are you going to do with them?"

"What's the matter?" Betty asked, rushing over to the table.

I hadn't meant to share my discovery with anyone but Mack, and I tried to signal him to be quiet.

He was too engrossed with an ivory button with a winged horse on it to notice. "I wonder if this could be valuable."

"What about buttons?" Betty asked.

"It's nothing, Betty."

But apparently she'd overheard the whole conversation. "I bet Les the Junk Man would know if they're valuable or not."

Les the Junk Man wasn't exactly the equivalent of Betty the Bag Lady, but close. He showed up every few months at the back door of the plant with a bunch of buttons, usually just shirt buttons and mother-of-pearl.

I had no idea where he found them, but he would offer the buttons to me for a couple of dollars. I always bought them from him for the extensive collection we already had in our repair and alterations department. Since we promised to replace buttons free of charge for our customers' clothes, you could never tell when the buttons would come in handy.

"Want me to try and find old Les?" Betty asked.

"No, Betty, I don't want you to go looking for him."

The last thing I needed right now was for Betty to go off on some wild-goose chase through the mean streets of Denver's underbelly. She'd done that once before, and it had sent Mack and me on a search-and-rescue mission that I had no desire to repeat.

"It wouldn't be any trouble," Betty persisted. "I bet he finds buttons like these all the time." She fingered one of the buttons—not a gem-type button but a silly one in the shape of a cow. Wouldn't you know?

"No, Betty," I said. "And besides, I know what Les would do if he found buttons like these. He'd sell them to me."

"Touché," Mack said as he took a bite from a ham sandwich out of his brown-bag lunch.

I didn't want to get into an extended conversation with Betty about the buttons. "Would you stop by my office when you're through eating, Mack?" I started to leave.

"Me, too?" Betty asked. "Can I come and look?"

"No. This is about a personnel matter I need to discuss with Mack." If she thought I was hiding something about the buttons, she'd become obsessed with finding out what it was.

She shrugged, but she didn't look happy. "I bet you guys don't know what Les's last name is."

"Excuse me?" I was halfway to the door.

"Les's name," Betty said. "It's Les Moore. Now ain't that a kick in the pants."

"Okay," I said, wanting badly to break away.

"You know, like in 'less is more.'"

"I got it," I said.

"Really," Mack said, obviously more interested in this conversation than I was. "That must have been why Les decided another person's trash would be his treasure."

"Yeah, like less *really* is more." Betty was so

pleased that Mack had appreciated her observation that she didn't seem to notice when I slipped away.

In my office, I continued to inspect the dresses while I waited impatiently for Mack. There was even a button that looked as if it was off an old army uniform. I didn't think it would be worth much since it seemed to be standard issue, the same as the ones that come on Levi's.

It wasn't long until Mack arrived. "Now, about this personnel matter you wanted to discuss." He had a smile on his face. "Betty, right?"

"She drives me nuts. Why does she always manage to get herself in the middle of things that are none of her business?"

"This time I would have to say that it really wasn't her fault."

"You're right. I should have looked around the lunchroom before I showed you the buttons."

Mack went over to the sofa where I'd laid out the dresses. "Now, let's take a look at the other buttons."

While he studied them, I filled him in on what I'd learned from Stan at the police department. All except the part about Stan's new girlfriend. I needed time to figure out how I felt about that.

"Stan said all of Thelma's doors were locked from the inside when she died and that the next-door neighbor swears that Thelma went down into the basement by herself all the time."

"Okay, there you are. The police didn't find anything suspicious about her death," Mack said.

Yeah, but I did, especially after finding the buttons, and I knew I had to talk to Thelma's neighbor before I'd ever be satisfied.

"But that still doesn't explain the buttons," I said. "I know some people collect antique ones. I wonder how much they're worth."

Mack smoothed out a final solid blue dress and gazed at its potpourri of buttons. "Worth enough to kill for? Is that what you mean?"

"I suppose. I need to find out."

"I have an idea where we can start."

I liked the fact that he said "we." It showed that he was as puzzled by the whole thing as I was.

"The woman who's handling the costumes for our play collects buttons. She might know something. I'll give her a call."

"Good idea," I said.

Mack was directing a theatrical production of Harper Lee's book, *To Kill a Mockingbird,* for his little theater group, and that would give him something to do while I did some undercover investigating in Thelma's neighborhood.

He started back to the cleaning department but ran head-on into Betty. I wondered if she'd been eaves-dropping outside the door all this time.

"Whoops," she said, recovering her balance immediately. "I got another idea. I thought of someone else who might know about buttons. He's a busker, and he used to work at the mall downtown but now he's up at the one in Boulder."

Betty's interest in the buttons was getting out of hand, the way Betty's interests often did. And besides, what the devil was a busker?

"Thanks, but we already thought of someone," I said.

Betty studied me for a moment. "You don't know what a busker is, do you, boss lady?"

Okay, so I didn't know what a busker was. A Husker, sure. Anyone in Colorado knew the Nebraska Cornhuskers were the University of Colorado's dreaded rival on the football field. So what if I didn't know about buskers?

Betty had a big grin on her face as she glanced at Mack. "She doesn't know, does she?"

"All right, so I don't know." My teeth were clenched together so tightly I could hardly talk. "Are you satisfied?"

Much to my irritation, Mack decided to join in. "By George, I think you're right." He winked at Betty. "I guess she just didn't get the proper education when she was kid."

"If one of you wiseacres wants to tell me, go ahead. Otherwise, why don't we all get back to work?"

Betty beamed. "A busker is a street entertainer."

Well, of course she would know that, being a former street person herself.

"And, as a matter of fact," Mack said, his voice taking on a professorial tone, "in 1938, Charles Laughton played a busker in a movie called *Saint Martin's Lane*—or, as it's also known, *Sidewalks of London*."

That explained how Mack knew the term. He was a movie buff without peer. In an ongoing game we had to try to fool each other with movie quotes, it was a red-letter day when I asked him a quote he didn't know.

"Well, thanks for that information," I said, anxious

to get rid of both of them. "I'm going up to the front counter now."

"But don't you want me to talk to the busker fella?" Betty said. "He's a juggler and a ventriloquist both, and he's got this cute little dummy, so I guess he's a double busker. Anyways, I figured he'd be able to help you out."

We were getting way off the subject now. "And what makes you think he knows anything about buttons?" I asked.

Betty looked triumphant. "'Cause he collects buttons and he wears them all over his clothes as decoration."

"Okay, Betty," I said, not wanting her enthusiasm to go completely unrewarded. "It's something to keep in mind."

"We could go to Boulder and talk to him."

The last thing in the world I wanted to do was go forty miles to Boulder to talk to one of Betty's buddies, but I tried hard to control myself. After all, I think one of the reasons I got so irritated with Betty was that I had the same tendency to butt in myself, at least according to some people. "Not now, Betty. Maybe later."

"But you don't even know his name?"

Like I couldn't find a juggler/ventriloquist in a button suit at Boulder's Pearl Street Mall. "Okay, what's his name?"

She snickered, and looked at me as if I were a bigger dummy than the busker's. "Well, what d'ya think it is? Buttons, of course."

Of course.

"You walked right into that one, Mandy," Mack

said, enjoying this conversation a whole lot more than I was.

"And this busker fella's dummy has ribbons all over his clothes. Bet you can't guess what his name is."

The way she said it, I figured it would be Mandy. I wasn't about to ask.

Mack played along with her, though. "No, what is it?"

"Well—duh—it's Bows. You know, like in that old song 'Buttons and Bows.'"

Mack laughed.

"Out," I said. I could hardly wait until they both left for the day so that I could start on some serious detecting.

FOUR

I HEADED UP FRONT to the call office. I'd left Ann Marie to work the counter alone, since her coworker, Julia, had called in sick that morning. Ann Marie was twenty-going-on-fourteen, and she always had an aura of general confusion about her.

I found her grappling with a roomful of customers, and I set about to help restore order. I even dispensed some free advice to a customer about how to remove perspiration stains from a beaded gown with a care label that said it couldn't be laundered or cleaned.

"If it's just the perspiration you're worried about, get some vodka and put it in a spray bottle," I said. "Then spray it on the stains. It will neutralize the smell, and you ought to be able to wear the dress again."

The woman looked at me as if I'd been nipping from a spray bottle myself, but she took the gown and left.

"I'm glad you got here when you did," my pony-tailed employee said. "I accidentally overcharged a man for his suit, and he said I was trying to take him to the cleaners. Now, isn't that weird? He was already here."

I explained to Ann Marie that "taken to the cleaners" was a phrase that meant someone was being cheated. It goes without saying that we dry cleaners hated it.

"Oh," Ann Marie said, looking as bewildered as ever.

But the conversation reminded me of Thelma again. She'd loved doing crossword puzzles and playing word games. She'd even brought me a Jumble out of the newspaper one time.

A Jumble is one of those puzzles where you have to rearrange letters to make four different words. Then, out of the circled letters in each word, you're supposed to come up with the caption for a cartoon. The Jumble she'd given me showed some characters playing a con game on a poor hapless victim. The answer, of course, was "Taken to the Cleaners."

After Thelma had done the puzzle—in ink, no less—she'd gone out and bought another copy of the newspaper just so she could give me the Jumble to work. Not being good at any kind of word puzzle, I had to get my newspaper friend, Nat Wilcox, to help me come up with the answer.

"I knew you'd get a kick out of it," Thelma said later. "Do you happen to know where the expression came from? It's so derogatory, and personally, I've always been completely happy"—she'd reached across the counter and patted my hand—"with my dry cleaner."

I'd wondered about the expression myself, at least in the few odd moments when I'd thought about it at all, and I'd promised to look into it for her. Sadly, it was still on my to-do list when she died.

Too bad Thelma hadn't circled a few letters in her

note about the bags of clothes that would have been a clue of some kind.

For the time being, my thoughts of Thelma had to be put on hold because the customers kept coming. People were bringing their woolen clothes out of storage to be cleaned in preparation for winter. One person even brought us a Donald Duck costume that she wanted cleaned for Halloween.

At one o'clock, Theresa, my afternoon counter manager, arrived to take over in the call office. Ann Marie had returned from lunch by then, so I headed back to my office to do some long-overdue paperwork. Mack waylaid me when I was almost there.

"I got in touch with the wardrobe woman on the play," he said. "She said she's just getting into button collecting and doesn't know that much about it."

Too bad. I might have to resort to one of Betty's usually unreliable sources after all.

"But never fear," Mack continued. "She said the woman you need to talk to is the president of her button club."

Button club? Button collectors were actually organized?

"Her name is Genevieve Atwood, and she agreed to see us at four o'clock if we can come out to her house."

That's when I'd planned to talk to Thelma's neighbor. If I didn't know better, I would have thought Mack was trying to foil my plans. However, maybe it would be just as well to wait until I could go there under the cover of darkness. I wouldn't want to run into Biker Babe.

MACK WATCHED ME climb empty-handed into his truck for the trip to the button club president's house.

"Aren't you going to bring any of the dresses?" he asked.

"I thought it would be better just to get a general overview about button collecting," I said. "I would rather not show anyone the dresses yet. I don't want people to get too interested in why Thelma had her button collection sewn on a bunch of old dresses until I figure it out myself."

"That's probably a good idea," Mack admitted as he steered the truck out of the parking lot and onto First Avenue.

"So where does this Genevieve Atwood live?" I asked.

He told me the address, in a high-income area with golf courses and country clubs. Maybe button collecting was a profitable hobby. Surely a person who lived in an area like that wouldn't collect something like matchbooks, which had no intrinsic value.

The leaves on the trees were beginning to change to their fall colors. I made a promise to myself to take time off and spend an afternoon in the park with my sketchbook before the leaves were all gone.

As Mack drove down Colorado Boulevard toward what I'd quickly come to think of as the Atwood estate, I kept up a running monologue about Thelma and the buttons.

"I wonder what the nephew is like," I said. "His girlfriend was kind of spooky."

Mack gave me an alarmed look. "Don't you go running off to see him. He might get suspicious of your motives."

It had been the last thing on my mind, but I realized I shouldn't have said anything about the girlfriend. Mack was slipping into the "protective parent" mode that he'd used with me when I was a kid hanging around the plant.

"Now promise," he said.

"Okay, I won't go see the nephew." I paused for just a beat. "By the way, do you know where the expression 'taken to the cleaners' came from?"

"And don't go trying to change the subject on me."

By then we were turning west on Hampden Avenue, the dividing line between Denver and the posh suburbs beyond. A few blocks later, Mack turned onto a residential street with expensive-looking homes. He made a right a block later and came to a stop in front of a rambling ranch-style house. Although not the estate I'd visualized, it was definitely in the upper-income category.

Surely the woman who lived here wouldn't collect inexpensive things like salt and pepper shakers. I was more hopeful than ever that Thelma's antique buttons would turn out to be valuable enough to convince Stan that the police should look into her death.

We climbed out of Mack's truck and walked up the sidewalk to the house. Mack rang the bell. An elegant fifty-something woman with enhanced blond hair and a golfing tan answered the door.

She was wearing a tweed skirt, a blue cashmere sweater set, a pearl necklace, and sensible two-inch heels without a scratch on them. I was glad I'd changed out of my uniform into a matching eggshell-colored sweater and slacks.

"I'm Genevieve," she said after Mack introduced us. "Won't you come in?"

She ushered us through a hallway past a formal living room to a family room at the back of the house. "Please have a seat," she said, motioning us to a chintz-covered sofa.

The room had a wide expanse of glass that gave us a panoramic view of the rolling fairways of a golf course and made me want to duck in case an errant golf ball came our way. Talk about living dangerously.

"Would you like a cup of tea?" she asked.

I shook my head, but Mack said yes, which was too bad because then we had to wait for her to play perfect hostess.

She finally came back with a silver tea service and a plateful of sugar cookies. "Didn't you bring the buttons?" she asked as she poured tea into a delicate china cup for Mack. "I understood from Harvest—"

Harvest? It took me a minute to realize that Harvest must be the name of Mack's friend. A throwback to the sixties, for sure.

"Harvest said you recently inherited a button collection and were wondering how much it was worth." Genevieve was looking at me.

"Yes," I said, "but I didn't really want to bother you with all the buttons. I guess I just wanted some information about buttons in general."

Genevieve nodded and dropped a sugar cube into her teacup, stirring it around with a tiny silver spoon. "Well, if you're looking for a huge fortune in buttons, my dear, you'll probably be disappointed, but the collection's value certainly could be in the thousands of dollars."

She'd read my mind and given me hope, all at the same time.

"Button collecting is the third most popular hobby in the country after stamps and coins—and, in fact, buttons have increased in value dramatically since the advent of Internet auctions.

"However, button collecting had a rather humble beginning. It didn't even become an organized hobby until the thirties. People were poor and couldn't afford to pursue expensive hobbies, but every woman had a button box and began to sort out the more unusual ones and assemble them into a collection. In fact, it was my grandmother's collection that got me started."

"Are there any buttons that are especially valuable?" I asked.

"Well, some people collect presidential buttons, and certainly the most sought after of those would be a George Washington button from one of his two inaugurations. A G.W., as we call them, would probably sell for several thousand dollars. French enamels are very expensive, and there's a set of hot-air balloon buttons from the eighteenth century that's worth more than ten thousand dollars."

I closed my eyes and tried to picture Thelma's buttons. I was quite sure there wasn't a presidential or a balloon button in the lot. I didn't know about French enamels.

"The nice thing about buttons is that you can begin to assemble a very nice collection for only a few dollars a button. Sometimes you find a treasure trove of buttons at a garage sale for next to nothing."

Somehow I couldn't imagine Genevieve—or Thelma,

for that matter—scavenging at garage sales in search of buttons.

Genevieve put that thought to rest. "I found one button at a garage sale that was worth several hundred dollars."

Well, there you go. That was more like it. If there were some hundred-dollar buttons in Thelma's collection, they could still add up to a sizable amount.

Genevieve's cheeks took on a rosy glow as she warmed to her subject. "Buttons are really antiques in miniature, and they're a delightful way to study art, history—whatever you want—about the world. In fact, almost every event of the French Revolution was chronicled in buttons from that period. They were worn by gentlemen of the time as political statements."

"By men?" I asked, wondering if I'd heard right and thinking of the bland buttons we were always having to replace on men's shirts.

"Oh, yes, dear. Originally, almost all buttons were worn by men, sometimes only for decoration, not to secure their clothes. Although archaeologists have found buttons that date from ancient Greece and Egypt, it wasn't until the Crusaders brought the idea of the buttonhole back from the Middle East to Europe that buttons began to be used in the way we think of them today."

I was stuck back on the thing about men. "But why not women?"

"It was kind of the peacock syndrome," Genevieve said, not as appalled as I was. "And after all, most women were hidden away in the home and didn't start wearing buttons—certainly not big or beautiful ones—until the middle of the nineteenth century.''

"That doesn't seem fair.''

"How about jewels?'' Mack interrupted, probably afraid I was going to get off on some feminist tirade. "Didn't some buttons have precious stones in them?''

"Yes, indeed,'' Genevieve said. "King Louis XIV was said to have spent the equivalent of six hundred thousand dollars on jeweled buttons. However, most of the buttons we find today are just cut glass or paste.''

She turned to me. "But you might be interested in this, Miss Dyer. Queen Victoria greatly influenced the buttons of her era. When she went into mourning for more than twenty-five years after the death of her husband, Albert, she never wore anything but black, including all the buttons on her clothes. They were made of jet, a coallike material. All the women of the time began to copy her, though their buttons were usually made of black glass.''

Genevieve wasn't through yet. "The charm of buttons is that every conceivable substance known to mankind has been used to make them. You might say that everything from A for aluminum to Z for zinc—including such odd materials as bread dough, chicken skin, and hair—have been used to make buttons.

"And it would be hard to think of an animal, vegetable, or mineral that hasn't been depicted on a button, especially on the wonderful picture buttons from the Victorian era. For instance, scenes and characters from Gilbert and Sullivan's operettas were popular subjects of buttons of the time.''

My mind had gone into overload, but fortunately

Mack asked a question. "What about the funny cut-out buttons—the ones with dogs and cartoon characters on them."

Genevieve laughed. "Oh, you mean goofies. Actually, we button collectors call them realistics today."

Well, no wonder Betty had gone for Thelma's button of a cow. It went along with the rest of her rather goofy personality.

"You know, it's interesting that you should mention them," Genevieve said. "A few of them are more valuable outside the field of button collecting. People collect them to go with other hobbies, rather like people who bought up the sheets of Elvis stamps because they collect Elvis memorabilia. And there are also some buttons called snap-togethers that come apart and are fun to collect."

I had a feeling that Genevieve could go on all night, and I waited for her to take a breath. "Did you ever know a woman named Thelma Chadwick?" I asked.

"Oh, is she the one who had the collection?"

I nodded, wondering if it was a wise idea to mention her name. "Was she ever a member of your button club?"

"Thelma Chadwick," Genevieve repeated. "The name does sound familiar. What did she look like?"

I described my elderly customer as best I could.

"And where did she live? She might have gone to one of the other clubs in the Denver area."

I was surprised to hear that there was more than one, but I gave her Thelma's address in east Denver.

"You know, one of our members lives in the same area. You could ask her. In fact, I remember now. I think Thelma might have come to one of our meetings with this particular member, but she never came back.''

Okay, that was a start—someone who knew Thelma and what her button collection might be worth. ''Do you have the woman's name and phone number?''

''I'll have to look up her number. I know it's unlisted.'' Genevieve rose from the chair where she'd been sitting across from us. ''By the way, she has a collection of presidential buttons, if you're interested.''

While she was gone, Mack helped himself to the last of the sugar cookies—just as I'd decided to have one. I got up and walked over to a mosaic on the wall. It had a kaleidoscope pattern and looked like a stained-glass window. When I moved closer, it turned out to be made of buttons. I realized there was a whole world of buttons out there that I knew nothing about.

As I started back to my seat, I glanced in the direction Genevieve had gone. I could see her on the phone inside a library filled with leather-bound books and leather-backed chairs. But the phone hadn't rung, so she must be calling someone.

I went back to the sofa and watched a foursome pass by on the golf course. It wasn't quite as boring as watching grass grow, but close.

''I'm so sorry,'' Genevieve said when she returned to the family room. ''I can't seem to put my finger on her phone number right now.''

I couldn't imagine that she'd misplaced it in this immaculate, orderly house. There wasn't even a magazine on the coffee table.

''Maybe you could just give me her name.''

"Don't worry. I'll look for the number and call you tomorrow if you'll give me your phone number."

I gave her my home number. No need to tell her where I worked since it was the repository of what could be a "treasure trove" of buttons.

She handed me a card with her own number on it and escorted us to the door. "If I can be of any more help, let me know," she said. "I'd love to take a look at the collection if you ever want to sell it."

I was still pondering her parting words as we got back in Mack's pickup. Maybe she'd known Thelma a lot better than she'd indicated and realized Thelma had a valuable collection. Then again, maybe it was my suspicious mind working overtime.

Mack pulled away from the curb. "So what do you think?" he asked.

"I'd say that it's going to take a lot more research to find out anything." I told him about seeing Genevieve on the phone. "Maybe she was checking with her friend and decided not to give me her number."

"Don't be so paranoid," Mack said. "Besides, Harvest said she has a book on buttons that she'll lend you. Why don't you stop by at rehearsal after work and pick it up?"

It was almost as if he knew I was planning a covert trip to Thelma's neighborhood and was attempting to keep me from it.

"I'll come by about ten," I said. "You should be winding up by then."

Mack looked at me as if he could read my mind. "Don't go snooping around that nephew in the meantime. Okay?"

"Okay," I said.

It was a good thing I hadn't mentioned Thelma's next-door neighbor. He probably wouldn't have wanted me to go there, either, but he couldn't object to what he didn't know.

FIVE

THE NEIGHBOR had told the police that Thelma went down into her basement all the time. Thelma had told me she didn't. Therefore, the logical thing to do was talk to the neighbor before I called Stan again.

I tried to think of how I should approach the woman. All I could think of were arguments Mack would probably give me for why I shouldn't go. I knew I had to go, anyway.

As soon as Theresa and I closed up the call office at seven o'clock, I climbed in my Hyundai and headed to east Denver. It was already dark when I drove out Sixth Avenue and then north on Monaco.

Thelma's house was near what used to be Stapleton Airport. When the city built its new runways and fancy terminal—Denver International Airport, or DIA—on the plains of eastern Colorado, Stapleton reverted to an empty expanse of land. It immediately became fodder for developers looking for new places to build offices and residential complexes.

In fact, when Thelma had told me that her landlord was selling the house she rented, I'd wondered if the real-estate values of the homes in that neighborhood had gone up in anticipation of a major building boom in the area. The new coat of paint I'd noticed the time I'd been there reinforced that idea.

She'd told me once that the TV used to flutter whenever a plane took off on one of the runways within spitting distance of where she lived. The property had to have appreciated in value once the noise pollution was gone.

When I reached her street, I parked halfway down the block and staked out her house. I could see Thelma's old black car in the driveway so I assumed Biker Babe and her boyfriend were home. I was hoping they would leave eventually, but not so I could follow them to see what they were up to. At least not yet. I just wanted to make sure they weren't home when I checked with Thelma's neighbor to the south.

I knew I might have to sit there all night, but within twenty minutes, I got lucky. I saw Biker Babe and a man I assumed was her boyfriend, Deke. They came out of the house, went around to the back, and then roared out the driveway on a monster Harley. Was I good or what—nicknaming the woman Biker Babe?

The guy I assumed was Thelma's nephew was just as scary as I'd imagined. He was tall, dark, and heavyset, and looked a little like Bluto, Popeye's adversary in the comic strip, or even John Belushi's character in *Animal House*. Take your pick. He was wearing black leather just like his girlfriend, and I could just imagine all the tattoos underneath his T-shirt that I hoped I never had an opportunity to see close up.

A nosy dry cleaner always has to have a cover when she goes snooping, and my plan, at least as much as I'd been able to think it through on the drive out there, hinged on Biker Babe's and Deke's not being home.

I waited until I saw them disappear around the corner on the Hog. Then I walked up to their door and rang the bell. That was just in case the neighbor to the south was looking out her window. Feigning disappointment, I crossed the yard, went around an old red-and-white convertible in the driveway, and up to the neighbor's door. A mail slot had the name Fitzgerald on it. A sign said her bell was out of order, so I knocked.

A man opened the door. He could have been the inspiration for one of the lowlifes in a Mafia movie. He was a skinny, thin-lipped little fellow who appeared to be in his forties, and he had atrocious taste in clothes. He was wearing a plaid jacket over a yellow shirt, plus lime-green pants and white shoes with a matching belt.

"Yeah, what d'ya want?" he asked.

This put me off my stride. When Thelma had talked to me about her prowler, I thought she'd said the neighbors on either side of her were either divorced or widowed women. I'd pictured them as elderly people like her.

"I—I wondered," I stuttered and took a deep breath. "I was wondering if you know if Deke Wolfe is still staying next door at his aunt's house."

"I got no idea. Let me get the lady of the house." He turned around and yelled toward a back room. "Hey, Naomi, will you get out here?"

"What is it, Frankie?" the woman yelled back. "I'm hurrying as fast as I can." She was trying to put on an earring when she got to the living room.

She looked a little older than he was, and even though her hair was a brassy blond color, it didn't fit her thin frame or her demeanor. She seemed overly anxious to please the man.

"There's someone here wants to know about the bum next door," Frankie said.

By then, the woman had noticed me. She came over to the door and smiled nervously. "Yes, what can I do for you?"

"I was looking for Deke Wolfe, Thelma's nephew. Do you know if he'll be back soon?"

"I'm sorry. I don't." Her eyes shifted nervously to Frankie. "They keep pretty much to themselves over there."

"Oh, really, I thought you were a good friend of Thelma's. Aren't you Naomi?" I was hoping she'd assume that Thelma had spoken of her often. In actuality, the only time I'd heard her name mentioned was when Frankie said it a few seconds before.

She nodded, seeming pleased.

"I was so sorry to hear of Thelma's death," I said.

Her smile disappeared. "Yes, poor woman. It was terrible to die that way."

"How was that? I'm afraid I never heard exactly what happened."

"She fell down her basement stairs," Naomi said, and gave a little shudder. "I spotted her body through a window and called the police."

"That's strange," I said.

"What d'ya mean—strange?" Frankie demanded.

"I thought she told me about a month before her death that she never went down in the basement anymore."

"You gotta be mistaken, lady. Naomi went down with her to the basement just a couple of weeks before she died. Isn't that right, Naomi?"

The woman nodded. "Yes, about that time, I guess."

"And we saw lights over there at night like she was working downstairs," Frankie said. "She was getting ready to move, you know."

"Are you sure it was only a few weeks before Thelma died that you were down in the basement with her?"

Naomi glanced nervously at Frankie and then back at me. "About then, I think. Maybe a little earlier."

I seemed to be at a dead end, and I grappled for something to keep the conversation going. "Were you helping her do her laundry?" I asked finally.

Naomi seemed to be waiting for a sign from Frankie on how to respond.

I plowed ahead. "Thelma told me she had trouble doing her laundry because the washer and dryer were down in the basement."

Naomi looked relieved. "Yes, that was it. She needed help with her laundry, and I couldn't help wondering if she'd tried to get down the steps with a load of clothes the night she died."

"We better get going or we're going to be late for dinner," Frankie said. "We're supposed to meet Buddy and Sal at Hooligan's at quarter to eight."

I thought perhaps he meant Houlihan's, but I didn't correct him. I'd never heard of a restaurant called Hooligan's unless it was a theme hangout for small-time hoods.

"All right, dear." She looked over at me as if she were pleading for me to understand. "I'm really sorry, but we have to leave."

"Want to give us your name and we'll tell the guy next door that you were here?" Frankie said.

"No, that's all right. I'll come back later." I got out of there as fast as I could.

I couldn't believe what had just happened. It was more than I had any right to expect.

Naomi was lying, but why had she played along with me? Why hadn't she been vague about the laundry, the way she'd been about the exact time when she'd been in the basement? After all, Thelma didn't do her own laundry anymore. Dyer's Cleaners did it for her.

SIX

I WAS ONLY A BLOCK from Naomi's house when it occurred to me that maybe I should follow the couple to Hooligan's—or whatever the name of the restaurant was where they were going. I hadn't had dinner, and I had a whole evening to kill before I was due to meet Mack at the theater.

Common sense prevailed. What could I hope to accomplish by going to Hooligan's? I probably wouldn't be seated close enough to overhear what they were saying, and if they spotted me, I would only make them suspicious of my interest in them.

Instead I waited in the next block until I thought they'd had time to leave, then circled back and parked in a different spot near Naomi's house. The red-and-white convertible was still in the driveway. If they were going to meet their buddy, Buddy, at a restaurant, they were certainly in no hurry to join him. It was after eight when they finally took off. I scooted down in my seat as soon as I saw them come out of the house. I waited until I heard them pull away and the hum of their motor fade before I looked up again.

Climbing out of my car, I hurried up to Naomi's door and knocked. It was the same procedure I'd used when I was supposedly looking for Deke and Biker Babe. This time I was hoping to find out what the neighbors had to say about Naomi. No one answered Naomi's door. Big surprise. I walked down from the porch, bypassed Thelma's place, and hurried to the house to the north. I rang the bell and waited.

I'd almost decided no one was home, despite the sound of a TV blasting away inside. Just then, a heavyset black woman with frizzy white hair opened the door. She fit the picture I'd had of Thelma's neighbors as widows and divorcees far better than Naomi had.

"Hi," I yelled. "I'm looking for a neighbor of yours—Naomi—" Fortunately, I remembered the name on the mailbox. "Naomi Fitzgerald. No one seems to be home at her place, and I was wondering if you know if she's gone out for the evening or is out of town."

"Naomi!" The woman harrumphed over the noise of the TV. "She's probably out gallivantin' with that no-good boyfriend of hers. Ever since she met him she's gone kind of crazy."

"Boyfriend? I didn't know she was seeing anyone."

"Oh, yeah. His name is Frankie. She met him at some honky-tonk bar, and ever since then, she's gone off the deep end."

"That doesn't sound like Naomi."

"Are you a friend?" the woman asked, still with her voice raised.

I swallowed hard and nodded. "A shirttail relative, actually, but I'm from out of town. I haven't seen her in years." My throat began to hurt from shouting, and in addition, I began to itch; it's an unfortunate habit I have when I go into prevaricator mode.

"Hmmm," the woman said.

For a minute I was afraid she was wondering why I'd said I hadn't known Naomi was dating someone if I hadn't seen her for such a long time.

Instead she asked, "Would you like to come in and see if she shows up? Can't promise when she'll be back, but maybe you'd like to have a cup of coffee and sit a spell."

I nodded again.

"Have yourself a seat over yonder, and I'll get the coffee." She waited for me to come inside, then closed the door, motioned to a sofa, and left the room, walking as if each step was painful for her.

I sat down where she'd indicated on a shabby tweed sofa and glanced around the room. It was equally threadbare except for a large television set that was tuned to a rerun of *Touched by an Angel*.

My hostess was entirely too trusting. Perhaps I should warn her about letting strangers into her house. Instead I picked up a copy of *TV Guide*. The mailing label was addressed to Willetta Woods. Was I shrewd or what—ferreting out the names of strangers from evidence in their homes? Perhaps I should go into the P.I. business.

Willetta came back to the living room with a couple of mugs of coffee. "I forgot to ask if you take cream or sugar."

"Nothing, thanks."

I put the *TV Guide* down on the table just in time for her to use it as a coaster. Then she sank heavily into a dark brown recliner, grabbed a remote, and turned down the sound on the TV. That was a relief.

"It's good to have company for a change," she said.

And of course, that must be why she was so careless about inviting a stranger into her living room. The poor woman was lonely.

"So tell me about Naomi's boyfriend."

"Oh, he showed up here a few months ago and moved right in."

Wasn't that about the time Thelma said she had the trouble with a prowler? My stomach clenched into a knot.

"Wouldn't be surprised if he has a record," she continued, "the way Naomi's so secretive about his past."

Good idea, I thought. I would have Nat Wilcox, my friend who was a reporter on the *Denver Tribune,* check on him. Only trouble was I didn't know the guy's last name.

Willetta must have read my mind. "Doesn't a name like Frank Pankovich sound phony to you?"

Actually, it sounded real to me. Frank Smith would have sounded phony.

"I call him Frankie Panky for short."

"As in hanky-panky, you mean?" I asked.

She gave a laugh and slapped her thigh. "Good one, girl. I'll have to remember that."

I took a sip of coffee, which was Starbucks-quality compared to the instant variety I had at home.

"What did you say your name was?" she asked. "I don't think I caught it."

Oh, damn. I tried to think desperately of a name that would sound legit to her, and as long as I'd started the charade, I had to keep it up.

"Bonnie—uh, Fitzgerald—a distant cousin, just passing through town."

"Bonnie. That's a nice name."

"I gather you and Naomi were friends before Frankie came into the picture," I said.

"Not so much. I was a better friend to my next-door neighbor, but she died."

"Oh, I'm sorry."

Willetta's eyes filled with tears. "We used to look out for each other, but my feet have been giving me so much grief lately that I haven't been able to get around the way I used to." She rubbed a swollen ankle above what looked like a man's bedroom slipper. "Otherwise, I might have found my friend before she died. She fell going down her basement steps and laid there for hours." A tear ran down her cheek, and she swiped it away. "If I'd been up and about, I might have been able to save her."

"I'm sorry," I said again. "Did she go down to the basement a lot?"

"Not that I knew of, but sometimes we old folks do foolish things." Yep, foolish things like letting a stranger into the house, I thought again.

"So who found her?" I asked, shaking off my urge to warn her.

"Well, once I got stove up, Thelma gave Naomi a key to her place, but apparently Naomi didn't use it. Just spotted her body through a basement window."

So Naomi had a key. This was getting more and more suspicious. I needed to keep Willetta talking about Thelma. But how—now that I'd said I was a relative of Naomi's?

"Maybe your friend thought she heard something in the basement and went down to investigate," I said.

Willetta nodded. "That's what bothers me. She'd seemed nervous about something just before she died, but she wouldn't tell me what it was. I guess she didn't want to worry me."

There wasn't any way I could tell her about Thelma's prowler since I supposedly didn't even know the woman.

"Maybe I should ask some of the other neighbors if they knew what was bothering her," Willetta said. "But enough about my problems. Tell me where you're from."

That caught me off guard. "Oh, a lot of places. I'm just passing through Denver on my way to California."

Willetta struggled to get out of her chair. "Say, would you like another cup of coffee?"

"Oh, no, I have to get going." But I felt so guilty about my lying that I stayed for a while just to keep her company. I shouldn't have.

"I really have to leave now," I said finally. "And please don't get up. I'll show myself out."

"I'll tell Naomi you were here."

"No, don't do that." I sounded panicky, but I tried to recover. "I want to surprise her."

She winked at me as if she understood and turned up the TV to its previous roar. The sound apparently shut out the rumble of Deke's motorcycle as he and Biker Babe, Leilani, rode into the adjoining driveway. They were only a few yards from me when I opened the door and walked out onto the porch.

They were arguing, and I didn't think Biker Babe

spotted me, but she certainly would if I tried to sneak down the steps and past Thelma's house to my car.

"On second thought," I said, "maybe I will take another cup of coffee." I slipped back into Willetta's living room. "But let me get us both a refill, okay?"

I went into the kitchen, as bare as the living room, and peeked out the window at the ruckus next door. The two leather-clad bikers were still going at it, but because of the volume on the TV, I had difficulty hearing what they were saying.

All I caught was the tail end of Deke's words— "...shouldn't have done that."

Call it my guilty conscience, but I wondered if they were arguing about the dresses she'd turned over to me? Would they be coming down to the cleaners to retrieve them tomorrow?

Biker Babe had gotten off the back of the motorcycle and was standing with her hands on her hips. She said something that sounded like "clear out." I didn't know if it was about her helping him clear out Thelma's stuff or clearing out of Denver.

She gave Deke a scalding look, then glanced over in my direction. I ducked behind the curtain, grabbed an old aluminum coffeepot from the stove, and poured the remains of the coffee from it.

As soon as I returned to the living room, Willetta turned down the sound on the TV again. Too bad she hadn't done it while I was eavesdropping. I handed her the mug of coffee and settled down on the sofa again, but I couldn't think of any more questions to ask.

Maybe that's why I decided I could no longer withhold my words of warning.

"You know," I said, "you really shouldn't be so trusting about letting people into your house. I could have been a thief for all you know and stolen something out of your kitchen while I was there."

"You're not a thief, are you?"

"Well, no."

"That's what I figured. I'm a pretty good judge of people, honey, and besides, you look just like that angel on TV." She motioned over to where Touched by an Angel was still playing. "The white one. And I look a little like Della Reese, don't you think?" At that, she laughed and turned so I could see her in profile.

"You know, you may be right," I said.

Actually, I thought we bore about as much resemblance to the "angels" as Mack and I did to Bill Robinson and Shirley Temple doing a tap dance routine in those old movies Mack liked so much. Still, the comparison to Roma Downey was flattering.

I stayed a while longer, and when I took the coffee mugs to the kitchen to rinse them out and stick them in a drainer, I snuck a quick look out the window. Deke and Biker Babe had apparently moved their argument inside.

I checked to see if my path was clear again as I said good-bye to Willetta and moved out to the porch. Then I bolted for my car under the cover of night.

It was almost nine-thirty by then, but I still had a few minutes to spare in order to get to the theater to meet Mack and the woman with the button book. I locked the doors, pulled on my seat belt, and started the car. Once in gear, I drove around the corner, where I stopped again. I pulled out my cell phone, a recent acquisition and far overdue, considering how many times I'd needed it in the past.

I punched in Nat Wilcox's home number. All I got was his latest answering machine message. It was a quirky entreaty to leave any tips that were "fit to print" as well as any salacious gossip that was for his "ears only." I'd known Nat since junior high, and the latter part of the message didn't mean much since Nat is a police reporter. He thinks everything is fit to print unless it's preceded by the words "off the record."

"Nat, this is Mandy," I said in a whisper when the beep sounded to leave a message. I realized that I sounded as if I thought someone was hiding in the backseat and raised my voice. "If you're there, Nat, please pick up." I waited a suitable length of time for him to get to the phone. "Okay, I guess you're not home. This is off the record, but I need you to do me a favor. Go to the newspaper morgue, or whatever it's called these days, and see if there's anything in your files about a man named Frank Pankovich." I took a guess at how to spell the last name. "I'll tell you about it later. Thanks." I cut off the connection but left the phone on in case he called me back.

It came in handy to have a best friend who was a police reporter, even if he was a pain in the butt sometimes.

I started the Hyundai again and headed out of the neighborhood. Unfortunately, it was a few minutes before I noticed the one-eyed car that started following me.

SEVEN

THE CAR WAS NEARLY a block behind me when I crossed Quebec, heading west on Colfax toward downtown.

At first, I didn't think anything about the fact that one of its headlights was out. I was too preoccupied with the information I'd learned about Naomi and her boyfriend, all of it highly suspicious and nerve-racking. In fact, it was probably because I was so jumpy that I even gave a thought to the car behind me.

There'd been a rumor that circulated in Denver several years ago about gang members who were driving around with only one headlight. Other drivers were warned not to blink their lights at any one-eyed cars or else they ran the risk of being shot at. It was supposedly part of an initiation rite for the gang and had become an urban legend that swept across the country.

I'd never heard of anyone actually getting fired at, but I shuddered just the same and hoped that no one would decide to warn the driver behind me that one of his headlights was out. I didn't want to be caught in the crossfire.

In fact, I decided to make a left turn and go south for a couple of blocks through a residential neighborhood to Thirteenth, a one-way street that would get me to Capitol Hill and the theater much more quickly anyway.

But darned if the one-eyed car didn't turn over to Thirteenth, too. Surely the car wasn't following me, but the talks with Thelma's neighbors had fueled my paranoia. I swung north on the next side street, east on Fourteenth, and north again, zigzagging my way back to Colfax. Ditto the car with the burned-out headlight.

And then I slammed the heel of my hand against my forehead a couple of times. Dumb me. It might not be a car at all. It could be Deke's motorcycle, which would mean that Biker Babe had spotted me as I left Willetta's house and she and her boyfriend were trying to see what I was up to.

I slowed, and the vehicle behind me did the same. It was still too far away for me to make out which one it was, a car or a motorcycle, but when I reached Colfax again, I hoped to be able to tell because it was better-lighted than the other streets.

I made a right turn on Colfax just as the light changed to red. This meant I was heading back toward Thelma's house, but I wanted to see if the vehicle would actually follow me the way we'd come. It squealed to the right through the red light, and I could see that it was a car with a ghostly right side that was draped in shadows from the faulty headlight.

That didn't necessarily exclude Deke and Biker Babe. They might be driving Thelma's old black sedan, or it could be Naomi and Frankie's convertible. I didn't wait to find out. My foot did a kind of tap dance as I pushed down on the accelerator, intent on losing them as fast as I could. Unfortunately, I caught the attention of a policeman as I sped by.

The patrol car tore out of another side street. I saw the lights flashing before I heard the siren. Just enough time for me to hope that the cop was responding to a call somewhere and wasn't after me.

Then the siren came on, and my hope faded. I pulled over to the curb and looked in the rearview mirror as the police car zeroed in on me. For just a second, I could still see the one-eyed car off in the distance. It appeared to have pulled over to the curb as well. Maybe this wasn't all bad, especially since the driver of the car apparently wasn't aware of the burned-out headlight. It made the vehicle easy to spot.

I flung off my seat belt in a vain attempt to get out of the car before the officer reached my window. I'd heard once that it was better if the person about to be ticketed got out of his car so he could be at eye level with the cop. But this guy was fast and wily. He made it to the window just as I was opening the door.

"This is a thirty-five mile zone," the young, round-faced officer said. "You were clocked doing forty-five." I'd apparently been caught with a radar gun.

I had to grip the steering wheel to keep from shaking. "I'm sorry, sir. I was afraid someone was following me, and I'm really glad you came along. I was trying to get away from that car back there." I gave a toss of my head.

"Where?" the cop asked, glancing in the direction we'd just come.

"Back there." I turned in my seat, but the cruiser now blocked my view of the one-eyed car.

I lifted myself up in the seat in an attempt to see

over the cruiser. I thought I spotted the car parked at the curb in the next block, but if it was my pursuer, it had doused its lights.

"I don't see it, lady."

"I'm sure it's still there. It had a broken right headlight, but the driver must have turned off his lights. I'd appreciate it if you would check it out. It was really scary."

"And have you drive off while I do?" He acted as if being tailed by another car was the lamest excuse in the world. "I'll check it out when I'm through. Now, let's see your driver's license and car registration."

Too bad. Here was an officer when I really needed one, and he was busy giving me a speeding ticket. It took me a good two minutes to find my registration buried in the debris in my glove compartment. Apparently, the cop spent the whole time bent over watching me in case I might be looking for a weapon. When I finally lifted my head, we were actually eyeball to eyeball, the way I'd wanted to be when I tried to get out of the car. He stood up, and I handed him the required cards and lifted up in my seat again. I could no longer see the mysterious car in the next block.

"What happened to the car back there?" I asked.

"It's gone."

He glanced up for a second, then back to the task of scrutinizing my license and registration. "Like I said, lady, I didn't see any car with a missing headlight."

"The driver must have slipped around the corner to Fourteenth with the lights off."

He shrugged and started writing the ticket.

The worst part was that I'd never been able to tell whether it was Thelma's black sedan, Frankie's red-and-white convertible, or simply a car with a malfunctioning headlight out for a joy ride.

At least if it had been the convertible, I figured Naomi and Frankie wouldn't know where to find me once they lost my trail. Unfortunately, Biker Babe did.

The policeman studied my license and registration as if I were driving a stolen car with an expired license.

Finally, he returned the license and registration and continued writing. "And I'm giving you a citation for not wearing a seat belt."

"But you can't do that."

He nodded as if he'd heard that argument before. "We can't stop you just for a seat belt violation, but if we stop you for another offense, it's completely within our authority."

I was practically babbling by then. "But I was wearing a seat belt when you pulled me over. I took it off before you got here."

"Sure, lady."

I sighed deeply and let it go. It just wasn't my night, and I figured I needed to pick my battles carefully. "Please keep your eye out for a car with a burned-out headlight. If you find it, maybe you can stop it and at least find out the name of the person who was following me."

"I'll certainly do that, ma'm." He looked at me as if I were Dr. Richard Kimble in *The Fugitive,* talking about the mythical one-armed man instead of a one-eyed car.

I didn't think it would do any good to point out that I tended to itch when I lied and I wasn't itching now. He probably would think that was the biggest lie of all.

Instead I started my car, and as soon as he pulled out from the curb, I took off after him. Just for a while and not exceeding the speed limit. Still, I wanted to have him within close proximity until I assured myself that no one was on my tail.

Finally I circled back toward downtown, keeping an eye out for any suspicious vehicles, either behind me or waiting in the dark on a side street. But apparently the cop had scared the one-eyed car away.

I was running late by the time I arrived at the theater. It had once been a movie house, but long before the big multiplex theaters were constructed, this little neighborhood cinema had fallen on hard times. It had been an art house for a while, and then it dabbled in porno flicks. Now the Capitol Hill Players called it home.

If it weren't for my run-in with the one-eyed car, I would have thought the gods wanted me to be here. There was a parking spot right in front of the theater. However, I didn't think this was the night to leave my car out in plain sight. I pulled around the corner and into a parking lot behind the theater.

I didn't know how shaken I was until I realized I was counting the cars and their locations in the parking lot, just in case any new ones, running without lights, pulled into the lot while I was inside.

Finally, after waiting a few minutes to see if anyone drove in after me, I decided the coast was clear. I climbed out of the car and ran to a door that led backstage.

"I'm looking for Mack Rivers," I said to a man who stopped me as soon as I got inside.

"Shhh," he said. "They're still rehearsing."

He was sitting in a chair and leaning over a wastebasket, whittling away at a bar of soap, and I was so puzzled I couldn't resist asking him what he was doing.

"It's for the play," he whispered.

I nodded, but I still wasn't sure what a bar of soap had to do with the Capitol Hill Players' production of *To Kill a Mockingbird*.

I'd always loved Harper Lee's book about Scout and her brother, Jem, and the summer they lost their childhood innocence but learned about prejudice and the real meaning of tolerance and courage from their lawyer father, Atticus Finch.

"The kids are supposed to find a couple of soap dolls in the hollow knothole of an old oak tree," the man said in a voice so low I could hardly hear him.

Now that he'd jogged my memory, I remembered that the children had begun finding little gifts inside the tree. Later they discovered that the trinkets were being left for them by Boo Radley, a strange man who had always frightened them but wound up saving Jem's life.

"Is it okay if I go out front?" I asked, keeping my voice down as well.

The man gave his silent approval, and I couldn't help thinking that he belonged onstage, wearing bib overalls and sitting in a rocking chair on a front porch in the 1930s Southern town where the play took place.

I slipped around him and let myself through the door that I already knew led to the front of the theater. I'd used it to get backstage often enough after one of Mack's many performances.

The house lights were down, which was a relief. I was hoping to be inconspicuous as I tiptoed up the aisle to a seat at the back of the theater. I didn't want Mack to realize I was late and get curious about where I'd been.

But suddenly my cell phone went off. Talk about making an entrance. I struggled to find it in my purse and turn the damned thing off. Mack didn't even turn around, just went on with the rehearsal, as I skulked into a seat.

The opening for the play was going to be this Saturday night, and I already had front row seats for it. I never missed one of Mack's plays, whether he was in front of or behind the lights. In fact, sometimes I thought if I didn't attend these theatrical productions, I'd have no social life at all. At least now that Stan and I had called it quits. But it was a new experience for me to see a rehearsal, almost as if the cast was giving a command performance just for me.

The actors were going over a courtroom scene in which a young black man named Tom Robinson was on trial—unfairly, as it turned out—for the rape of a white woman. Atticus was defending him, which had turned the white community against Atticus and made his children wonder why he'd taken the case.

"Sam, you need to project a little more." Mack's voice boomed from his seat up near the stage. "This is your closing summation, and you need to make it more dramatic."

Too bad Mack couldn't play the part of Atticus. With his deep voice and dignified stature, he'd be wonderful in the part. Except he was the wrong color. And he was too old to play Tom, but I was sure he would have stolen the show in the part if he'd been younger.

The actors ran through the scene one more time, and then Mack announced that everyone could go home. "We'll meet back here at six-thirty tomorrow night, and I'm sorry the rehearsal ran late tonight."

I glanced at my watch. It was already quarter to eleven. I hadn't realized that my run-in with the one-eyed car and the cop had taken so long.

The crew headed offstage, and I got up and started down to the front of the theater. It had been my hope that Mack would think I'd been sitting in the back of the auditorium for hours, despite the ringing phone, but he must have noticed me sneak up the aisle. Not to mention that he had eyes in the back of his head, the way he did at work so he could see that the crew didn't slack off on the job.

"Where you been?" he asked as I approached, not even bothering to look at me. "The actors were beginning to get restless because I kept them here so long waiting for you to show up."

Whoops. I was in trouble, and I tried to shift Mack's attention to something else.

"As the director, I would have expected you to be wearing a cape or at the very least a beret," I said.

Mack did glance up then. He gave me a look that said the remark wasn't worthy of a response. "So what have you been up to?"

I tried a different tack. "Why didn't you let me

carve the soap dolls? I'm an artist, after all.'' Or at least I'd always thought of myself that way until the press of work interfered once I inherited the cleaners from my uncle.

I could tell my question about the dolls put Mack on the defensive, but before he had a chance to answer, a woman approached. She was carrying a huge book, and her flamboyant attire suggested that she must be the person in charge of costumes for the Depression-era play. Except she looked as if she were a few generations removed. A flashback to the sixties in a long, bright tie-dyed skirt, a fringed blouse, and sandals. The whole ensemble was set off by a necklace made of various-sized mother-of-pearl buttons.

Mack introduced me as the person who was interested in learning about buttons. "And this is Harvest."

Yes, she was a real product of the sixties, right down to the name that her hippie parents must have saddled her with. She looked to be in her mid-thirties, the same as me, and she had long brown hair almost to her waist that had gray strands in it.

"Hi," she said. "I told Mack that I'm just getting into button collecting and don't know that much about it. Mainly, I like to make jewelry out of buttons." She fingered her necklace and flung back her hair to show off matching dangle earrings.

I thanked her for directing us to Genevieve Atwood, the button club president.

"Isn't she wonderful?" Harvest said. "She's the one who told me about this book on button collecting, and I'll be glad to loan it to you. It'll probably tell you more than you ever want to know about buttons." As if Genevieve already hadn't.

"Thanks," I said. "And I'll take good care of it."

"Now, let's get out of here," Mack said. "It's getting late." He motioned for us to follow him up onto the stage and into the wings. Most of the other people had already departed.

"Be sure to lock up, Jimmy," he said to the soap whittler as he held the door for Harvest and me to go outside.

Several cars I'd noticed earlier still remained parked up next to the building, but there was one new car, its lights out, in the shadows of a tree at the back of the lot. Maybe I hadn't been as smart as I'd thought I was about shaking the one-eyed monster. I felt myself tense despite my efforts to control myself.

"Hey, would you guys like to get something to eat?" I asked, suddenly nervous about going to my car and driving home alone. "Maybe we could go in your pickup, Mack."

I could see Mack give me a suspicious look in the dim light from above the stage door. As an actor, he'd learned all the slight nuances of body language that convey emotions. "You mean you haven't had dinner yet? What were you doing all this time?"

"It was just a thought."

"Sorry, I can't," Harvest said. "I see my old man is waiting for me."

With that, she headed for the car at the back of the lot, the one that had set my nerves on edge and made me tender the invitation in the first place.

Damn, now that I knew it wasn't the one-eyed pursuit vehicle from earlier in the evening, I wanted nothing more than to jump into my own car and go home. But Mack was on to me.

"Sure, I'll go get dinner with you, Mandy," he said. "Something tells me you've been up to no good."

EIGHT

WHEN WE'D SETTLED DOWN at a booth in an all-night diner, Mack got right to the point.

"So why were you late getting to the theater? What were you up to earlier?"

"What makes you think I was up to something?"

"Well, for one thing, you're beginning to itch."

I looked down at my lap, where my right hand was scratching my left palm, which was his tip-off that I was being evasive, if not downright deceitful. "You know, Mack, sometimes an itch is just an itch."

I didn't think he was buying my explanation, but apparently he was willing to let it go until we ordered.

Meanwhile, I opened Harvest's button book, so large it looked as if it should be on a stand in the reference section of a library. "Look," I said, "doesn't this look like one of Thelma's buttons?"

I pointed to a brass button with the French fleur-de-lis on it. Mack turned the book around toward him just as a gray-haired waitress approached. "Need a menu?" she asked.

I shook my head. All I wanted to do was eat and get out of there before the Grand Inquisitor had a chance to grill me too much. "I'll take a cheeseburger with fries and a cup of coffee."

"That'll work for me, too," Mack said, and continued to stare at the picture. "It doesn't look like any of the buttons I saw, but I didn't really have time to look at all of them."

Well, actually it didn't look like any I'd seen, either, but at least it was a temporary diversion that got Mack off my back.

He flipped through the book. "These must be the balloon buttons that Grace Atwood said were so valuable," he said, scooting the book around to me again.

The series was an eighteenth-century depiction of man's early attempts to fly, including one that said "Joke of the Century" in French. "Even if the set was worth ten thousand dollars, who could ever collect all twelve?"

The waitress returned with our coffee, and I continued through the book, making innocuous comments as I went so that Mack wouldn't have a chance to interrupt with questions about my whereabouts earlier in the night.

I noticed a collection of buttons about cats. "'Cats were not the subject of as many buttons as were dogs, and today command a higher price from collectors,'" I read, then thought of my own grouchy feline at home and glanced at my watch. "I wish the waitress would bring our meal. Poor old Spot hasn't had anything to eat all day."

Whoops. Wrong thing to say.

"Which reminds me," Mack said, "I don't think you ever answered my question about why you were late to the theater."

I was quick, if not necessarily good, with a retort. "And you never answered the question I asked this afternoon about the origin of the expression 'taken to the cleaners.'"

"Oh, you really wanted to know," he said. "Well, as a matter of fact, I do know." As a quid pro quo, I was sure he'd expect me to explain my whereabouts earlier in the evening. "The derivation is kind of vague, but apparently it has nothing to do with dry cleaners."

The waitress came back right then, bearing two burger platters. Maybe if I ate fast, I could get out of there while Mack was still talking about the origins of everyday phrases.

"It's of a relatively recent usage," he said, his voice taking on the same professorial tone he'd used when he'd mentioned the Charles Laughton "busker" movie to Betty and me earlier. "It dates back to the 1930s, when a lot of people were losing their money in bank failures and business deals gone bad."

That same pesky era when button collecting got its start. I nodded to urge him on and took a big bite of my cheeseburger, not even stopping to put ketchup and mustard on it.

"It actually had to do with a nineteenth-century expression, 'to be cleaned out,' which meant to be duped of all one's money." He stopped abruptly. "So now it's your turn."

I swallowed and tried to look as if I'd had a bright idea. "Maybe we dry cleaners should take advantage of the term, derogatory or not. You know, we could start an advertising campaign: 'You'll never be taken to the cleaners at Dyer's.'"

Mack gave me a frosty look. "And getting back to the subject of your late arrival..."

He was definitely wearing me down. Besides, I was bursting to tell someone what I'd learned, but I needed to find a friend who would be nonjudgmental and unconcerned about my safety.

What was I talking about? I already had such a friend—my newspaper buddy, Nat, who didn't care a hoot what I did. The only trouble was that, if the information had anything to do with crime, he wanted to record every gory detail on the front page of the morning paper.

"Okay," I said finally. "I didn't visit Thelma's nephew, if that's what you're worried about, but I did go talk to a few of her neighbors, and I found out some interesting things." I took another bite of cheeseburger.

"So are you going to tell me or not?"

Frankly, the information was too good to keep, so I spouted all my suspicions about Naomi, the next-door neighbor, and her boyfriend, Frankie. "She claims she spotted Thelma's body through a basement window and never went inside the house even though she had a key. At the same time, her boyfriend says she went down into the basement with Thelma just a few weeks before she died."

"Maybe she did," Mack said.

"But you haven't heard the best part. I asked if she was helping Thelma do her laundry, and she said yes. But remember how I said Thelma had us do it for her."

Instead of giving me a verbal pat on the back, Mack looked appalled. "And how long do you think it's going to take the couple to wonder why you were asking so many questions?"

Unfortunately, maybe they already had, but I chose to ignore that point. "What I'm wondering," I said, "is whether Naomi and Frankie knew about Thelma's buttons, and killed her for them, but then couldn't find them."

Before I could continue, the waitress was back with a refill on our coffee.

Mack waited until she left. "So what were you so spooked about in the parking lot just now?"

Like I said, he never misses a thing, and I was too tired to come up with a suitably creative fib, even if it was to protect him from worrying about me.

"Well, if you must know, I thought someone was following me after I left Thelma's street. There was this one-eyed car—you know, with one headlight burned out. It kept turning every time I did."

Mack began to tut-tut with his tongue. "So you think Naomi and Frankie are on to you already."

"Either that or Biker Babe and her boyfriend, Deke. It's possible they saw me when I was coming out of another neighbor's house but I couldn't tell if the car was Thelma's black sedan or Naomi and Frankie's red-and-white convertible."

"Dammit, Mandy, you shouldn't go snooping around like that."

"But if I'm going to make a good argument to Stan for the police to investigate Thelma's death, I have to have something to base my opinion on."

"Are you telling me that you think this so-called one-eyed car followed you to the theater?" Mack asked.

I shook my head. "Only for a minute, until I realized the car at the back of the lot belonged to Harvest's boyfriend. I'm almost certain I lost the one-eyed car."

"But you can't be sure?" Mack looked grim, as if he were settling into a Mandy-induced depression.

I tried to lighten his mood by relating my story about the cop, attempting to make the incident a whole lot funnier than it really was. I even embellished on how I'd tried to unfasten my seat belt so that I could get out of the car and be on the same level with the cop.

"By the time the cop got through ticketing me, the car had disappeared," I concluded. "And do you know the guy actually had the audacity to cite me for not wearing a seat belt."

"Just pay the two dollars," Mack said, chuckling as he made what I thought was a totally inappropriate remark.

"What do you mean—pay the two dollars? It's going to cost a whole lot more than two dollars."

"I didn't mean that. It's a quote from a movie. Don't you recognize it?"

Oh, yeah, as if I felt like playing our trivia game about movie quotes right now. At least I'd diverted his attention, but I had no idea where the quote came from. "Sorry, I don't recognize it."

"Haven't you ever seen *North by Northwest* on late-night TV? Cary Grant gets mistaken for someone else, and he's kidnapped and taken to a mansion on Long Island where he's forced to drink 'this much' bourbon." Mack stretched his arms straight out as far as he could reach and almost hit the waitress, who was back to top off our coffee. "Oh, sorry," he apologized.

"Don't worry," she said. "You didn't even touch me, and I sure remember that movie. I loved the part in the cornfield where the crop duster was trying to kill poor Cary."

Mack nodded. "One of the great scenes in movies."

Before they could get into a discussion of old Hitchcock movies, I interrupted. "No more coffee for me."

Mack put his hand over his cup. "None for me, either."

The waitress looked as if she'd like to stay and take part in the conversation, or at the very least sit down and give her feet a rest, but she finally left.

"So what does Cary Grant have to do with my speeding ticket?" I asked.

"Well, the bad guys in the movie put Cary behind the wheel of a car, then follow him, hoping he'll drive over a cliff, but a cop spots him and pulls him over. The bad guys make a U-turn and disappear, just like your one-eyed car."

I nodded. "Okay, but what does that have to do with the two dollars?"

"Cary's mother didn't believe his far-fetched tale about people getting him drunk and putting him behind a wheel, and she finally said 'Just pay the two dollars.'"

I knew I was getting a little snippy, but I was tired and I wanted to get home now that I realized there was no one-eyed car waiting in the theater parking lot to follow me there. "And the moral is?"

"Be glad the cop came along when he did—and quit snooping around."

"And did Cary quit snooping around?"

"No," Mack admitted. "He took the police back to the mansion the next day."

"So maybe that's what I should do."

"There was no evidence that he'd ever been there, and he finally winds up in South Dakota, sliding down the faces on Mount Rushmore."

"That part I remember."

"So let that be a lesson to you," Mack said as if the subject were closed.

All it did was make me realize I shouldn't go to the police yet. Better I should go back to Thelma's neighborhood alone the next night and see which couple would leave their house in a car with only one headlight.

NINE

I LUGGED THE BUTTON BOOK up to my apartment on the third floor of an old Victorian house in the Capitol Hill area of Denver, close to downtown and a few blocks south of Colfax.

I was almost there when I noticed someone sitting on the landing in front of my door. I came to an abrupt stop, afraid for a split second that it was the driver of the one-eyed car.

"Yo, Mandy."

Only one person I knew used slang, even in his greetings, so I proceeded up the stairs. "Hi, Nat. You must have gotten my message. Were you able to find out the information I wanted?"

He jumped up from the landing. "What message? What information?"

Okay, if he wasn't here about the message, he was probably here to schmooze, but he didn't usually do that so late at night.

"What message?" he repeated as soon as I reached the top of the steps. I unlocked the door to my apartment. It's what I call my "artist's studio," although I seldom have time to paint. Spot, my grouchy but hungry cat, was waiting for me. That's the only time the feline pays me the attention I deserve.

"First, tell me why you're here," I said. "That'll give me a chance to feed Spot."

I'd inherited Spot from my uncle, who'd named the cat in honor of the stains we removed from clothes. I think Spot resented the name, but my uncle had always maintained that the reason the cat was so bad-tempered was that the poor thing had arthritis.

"What ya got?" Nat asked, curious about the huge book I was holding.

I thrust it at him, sure he'd be bored with it in thirty seconds. By the time I finished filling Spot's food dish and getting him fresh water, Nat had cast the book aside. "I've been trying to call you all night," he said. "I think I've finally found the girl of my dreams, Man."

I tried to ignore his shortening of my name, but I couldn't help rolling my eyes at his proclamation. How many times had I heard that he was in love?

"I bet she's tall, blond, and gorgeous. Right?"

"How'd you guess?" Nat asked, knowing full well that all his broken romances—and his path was littered with them—had been with tall, buxom blondes. "But this one tops them all."

"So, what does that make her—six feet tall?"

"No, she's only five-ten." Nat gave me a disgusted look over his wire-rimmed glasses. "What I meant is that she's really hot. She's a Broncos cheerleader."

I handed him a beer that I didn't even bother to ask if he wanted. I knew he would. "When are you going to learn? She'll break your heart and then you'll come crying to me about it the way you always do." I sat down beside him on my sofa, which doubles as my bed when it's pulled out.

I kept telling him to shoot lower, someone who was at least shorter than his five-feet-eight. But Nat, who looks a little like John Lennon with those glasses, never listened to me. I'd already told him he should cut his hair—that the Beatles image he liked to project wasn't the girl magnet he thought it was. I was happy to see that he'd been keeping his hair trimmed these days, even if it was still too long, but I didn't know how much that counted with a woman who was surrounded by tall, handsome football players.

"Well, I hope it works out." I was sure Nat was headed for heartache, but after all, he'd been supportive—more or less—of my relationship with Stan Foster, even though he and the homicide detective had a natural antagonism to each other. And he'd been there for me when I broke up with Stan, telling me I'd done the right thing.

I almost started to ask him if he knew that Stan was going with a kindergarten teacher now, but at the last minute I thought better of it. No need to tip him off right now that I'd talked to Stan.

"So what is this information you wanted me to look up?" he asked.

"I wondered if you could check the newspaper files and see if there's any information about a Frank Pankovich." I spelled out the last name just as I had on Nat's answering machine.

"Why?" He eyed me suspiciously.

I'd known that he would want an explanation, and it was a fair question considering the fact that I'd requested his help. However, I wasn't yet ready to tell him I suspected that a customer of mine had been murdered. He would bug me about it all the time if I did.

"Well," I said, "I met this guy, Frank, and he's very interesting, but I'm—" How did I phrase this so my request wouldn't get him too curious? "I'm just not sure he's on the up-and-up."

Nat got a silly grin on his face. "Aha. So you've decided to start dating again."

I was surprised at his leap in logic, but of course, that's what he would think since we'd been discussing his new romantic interest in a cheerleader. Come to think of it, this might work out better than anything else I could come up with on the spur of the moment. However, I have to admit that the thought of being romantically involved with Frankie made me want to lock myself in my apartment and throw away the key.

"So where'd you meet this guy?"

"Uh—he was an acquaintance of one of our customers."

"Okay, but what makes you think he should be checked out?"

"I don't know. He just seems to have a mysterious past."

"That ought to be a red flag right there." Nat got up and started to pace. "You should drop the guy pronto. Presto. Abracadabra. Make him disappear. I'm telling you this for your own good."

Why, oh why, hadn't I said I was checking on him for one of my customers? "Would you just check him out, okay? See if he's ever been in trouble."

Nat stopped and stared at me. "You're really serious about this guy, aren't you?"

I started itching and stuttering at the same time, and the only thing I could think to say was "I—I call him Frankie Panky."

"Awgh," Nat said, sounding for all the world like a dying parrot. "I've never heard you be this dopey over anyone. You really must be nuts for the guy." Nat looked as if he wanted to gag.

I felt that way myself, but what could I do once I'd gotten myself into this predicament?

"So what's he call you—Mandy Pandy?"

I glowered at him. "Just shut up and do it, Nat, or I'll never speak to you again."

"Okay, I'll do it, but I have to meet this guy."

Not if I could help it. I rushed Nat out of my apartment, leaned against the door, and scratched.

"DO YOU KNOW WHY men's clothes always button on the opposite side from women's?" I asked Mack as I came through the back door the next morning.

"No, but I'm sure you're going to tell me."

"It started in the Middle Ages so that men could unbutton their coats with their left hands while they were pulling out their swords with their rights."

"I gather you learned that from the button book."

I didn't admit to Mack that this was about the only thing I'd learned about buttons before I fell asleep. Now I was ready to study the book because I could compare its pictures of buttons with the ones on Thelma's dresses.

Before I could do that, I had to spend the first few hours working the counter. Then I took over at our shirt press because the woman who normally handles the shirts had to take her son to the doctor.

Unfortunately, that put me in close proximity to Betty, who kept our washers and dryers running.

"Did you find out anything about those buttons?" she asked.

"It's going to take a while."

"Well, me and Artie just happened to run into Les Moore yesterday afternoon, and he said he'd be over here in a day or so to take a look at them."

I swore under my breath. All I needed was to have a ragman analyze the buttons. And I'd be willing to bet that Betty had talked Arthur, her doll doctor boyfriend, into helping her hunt for Les. Why did Arthur, who looked like an aging Kewpie doll, put up with Betty's escapades, much less participate in them?

"Look, I prefer to go to an expert for my information, if you don't mind." I slapped a shirt onto the shirt press and pushed a lever to apply steam. I felt as if it were coming right through the shirt and out my ears.

"Well, you can't find no expert that knows his junk better'n old Les," Betty said.

I tried to ignore her for the rest of the shift, but it was hard to do. She kept telling me about all the things Les had found to furnish her apartment, including one particularly ugly green ceramic dragon that I'd had the misfortune to see for myself.

At three o'clock, I finally escaped to my office. I checked my answering machine at home to see if Genevieve Atwood, president of the button club, had left a message about the member who lived in Thelma's neighborhood. To my surprise, she had. She said the woman's name was Mitzi Porter and gave me her phone number.

"I wanted to check with her before I gave out her

number," Genevieve said in her gracious, country club voice. "I hope you understand."

Why hadn't she just said at the time that she didn't give out a member's number without her permission? Was it just good manners, which I'm sure Genevieve had in abundance, or had she wanted to talk to Mitzi first so they could get their stories straight?

Stop it, Mandy, I thought, giving myself an imaginary slap in the face for what Mack called my paranoia.

I called the number and set up an appointment with Mitzi. She turned out to have a little-girl voice to go with her name. I was sure it was attached to a shy, retiring kindergarten teacher who used that voice to keep her five-year-old charges under control. Okay, maybe the reason I thought that was because I was trying to put Stan's new girlfriend in the most unfavorable light possible.

I gave myself another imaginary slap and explained to Mitzi that I didn't get off work until seven. I asked if I could visit her after that.

"I guess so, as long as Genevieve thinks it's okay." I could hear the hesitation in her voice.

"Oh, Genevieve thinks it's a wonderful idea," I said. "What's your address?" She gave it to me, and I hung up before she could change her mind.

Once that was accomplished, I opened the button book. I had an hour before I had to go up front to help with the after-work rush.

I grabbed the sandwich Mack had brought me from his lunch hour run to a deli and started going through the book. It soon became apparent that I wasn't going to find an exact match to any of Thelma's buttons without a lot more scrutiny.

For one thing, the book indicated that most buttons before the mid-nineteenth century were custom-made for the gentry of the time. For another, literally millions of buttons had been mass-produced after the start of the Industrial Revolution, so the chances of getting an exact match were probably greater than the odds of winning the Colorado lottery.

I considered drawing some sketches of the more interesting buttons in Thelma's collection, but what good would it do to show them to Mitzi? Who could tell what kind of material they were made from or if the gems were imitations? I finally decided my project for tomorrow, providing my employee on the shirt press was back, would be to remove some of the most interesting of Thelma's buttons and seek advice from an expert in the field. But probably not Genevieve.

I started inspecting each garment carefully, something I hadn't done before. When I got to a blue shirtwaist with big pink roses on it, I noticed a lump along the hem. On the wrong side of the dress, sewn to the hem, were a couple of brass buttons that looked like street signs.

The reason they caught my attention and brought a chill to my spine was that they had the words ''Danger'' and ''Proceed with Caution'' imprinted on them.

TEN

ONLY THE HOUSE in the block had on its porch light. I decided that must be where Mitzi Porter lived.

The two-story house appeared to have brown siding that made it merge into the surrounding night. Either that or it was badly in need of a paint job. Even the overhead light didn't reflect off the background enough so that I could see the street address. Mitzi had said it was on a shingle above the front door.

The structure looked as if it might once have been a farmhouse in the days before Denver spread out from the core city. It was certainly a far cry from Genevieve Atwood's expensive ranch-style home overlooking a golf course, but it was just a block away from where Thelma had lived. This gave me hope that Mitzi had known my friend and maybe was familiar with her button collection.

The floor of the porch creaked when I stepped on it, and I almost tripped on a warped board. When I righted myself, I knocked rather than fumble around for a bell.

I half expected Mitzi to open the door on a chain or at least look out a peephole at me. Her soft, tentative voice made me picture a nervous person who'd want to see some identification before she let me inside.

Instead, a heavyset woman opened the door without a moment's hesitation. She appeared to be in her mid-fifties, had steely gray hair pulled back in a bun, and looked as if she'd been an opera singer in a former life. I'm talking about the one who inspired the phrase "It's not over till the fat lady sings."

Maybe I had the wrong place. "I—I was looking for someone named Mitzi Porter," I said. "I must have the wrong house." I was already beginning to back away from the door.

"I'm Mitzi," the woman said in the little-girl voice I recognized from the phone. It went with her size about as well as a Southern accent would have gone with a Chicago mob boss. In all fairness, she was stout, not fat, and with an hourglass figure, providing hourglasses came in the large economy all-day size.

I introduced myself, still not able to reconcile the difference between her sound and her size. Her ample bosom seemed as if it would surely house a diaphragm that would project a stronger voice, one that could sing the lead in a Wagnerian opera and never get winded. I needed to forget the opera singer comparison, but Brunhilda would have been the name I would have chosen for her.

Once she invited me into her living room, which was clean but cluttered, she insisted that I have some coffee and cake. "I went to the store and bought a coconut cake especially for you," she said. "I hope you like it."

Coconut cake wasn't my favorite, but I couldn't very well refuse a piece after that. I sat down on the sofa, a worn Early American model with rocking horses and grandfather clocks on the fabric, and waited for Mitzi to return from the kitchen.

When she finally appeared with the cake and coffee on a tray, I didn't waste any time. After all, my second reason for coming back to Thelma's neighborhood was clandestine in nature. I wanted to stake out Deke and Biker Babe as well as Frankie and Naomi next door to see if either couple might drive away in a one-eyed car.

"Genevieve Atwood said she thought you brought a woman named Thelma Chadwick to a button club meeting one time," I said.

"Oh, she was wrong about that." Mitzi fluttered her hand in front of her face. "I told Genevieve I remembered talking to her at one of our meetings, but I didn't bring her there."

I wondered why my hostess hadn't told me that on the telephone, but I persisted. "Did you happen to know her from the neighborhood? She lived over in the next block."

Mitzi shook her head, tiny little movements to go with her voice. "She told me that at the meeting, but I was never at her house. It's a dark old place over on the next street, isn't it?"

I thought that was a rather unkind remark. To use one of Nat's everlasting clichés, it was kind of like the pot calling the kettle black. Mitzi's house wasn't anything to shout about with its brown siding. Of course, I hadn't known what Thelma's house looked like before the owner fixed it up to sell it. All I remembered was that it had a fresh coat of white paint the day I helped Thelma get the old clothes out of her basement for our clothing drive.

"To tell the truth," Mitzi said, "I had hoped maybe the two of us could get acquainted, but she didn't seem interested. People move in and out of this neighborhood so fast that it's sure hard to make any friends."

Maybe I should introduce her to Thelma's neighbor Willetta. Both of them seemed lonely. Otherwise, why would either one of them let me into her home so readily?

"Genevieve says that Thelma passed away and you inherited her button collection," Mitzi said, taking a big bite of cake.

"Well, yes, but I don't know much about it."

"I'd be glad to take a look at it if you want me to."

I might consider taking her up on the offer once I assembled the buttons in some sort of display. At least she wasn't offering to take them off my hands the way Genevieve had. I took a sip of coffee and decided to give her a test.

"Maybe you could tell me about a couple of buttons. Thelma had several that look like street signs. I don't know anything about them, but they seemed interesting."

Mitzi closed her eyes for a minute as if trying to visualize the buttons I described. "You know, I may just have some pictures of a set like that in one of my books. Hold on."

She got up easily from the other end of the sofa, her weight not seeming to be a hindrance, and I thought of how poor Willetta had struggled out of her chair. If I introduced them, maybe Mitzi could be of some help to the ailing black woman on the next block. I would have to give it some serious thought.

Mitzi went over to a dining room table, piled high

with books and papers, and started going through them. I probably shouldn't have asked her about the buttons. Now that I realized she really didn't know Thelma, I was anxious to get over to the next street to start my surveillance.

I sipped coffee and took several bites of the coconut cake so I would be ready to make a fast exit as soon as she found what she was looking for.

It took her so long that I'd eaten the cake and emptied the coffee cup by the time she pulled out a book and started leafing through it. I was about to tell her to forget the whole thing when she stopped and smiled triumphantly.

She returned to the sofa and sat down beside me. "Is this what they look like?" She handed me the book. "They're brass buttons from a set."

I nodded, recognizing the two buttons that warned of danger and urged caution. The others in the set weren't in Thelma's collection: "Soft Shoulders," "Curves Ahead," "Slow Down," "Dead End," and "Stop." If Thelma had been playing a game with me, the fact that "Slow Down," "Dead End," and "Stop" were missing could be significant. I chose to ignore "Soft Shoulders" and "Curves Ahead."

I handed the book back to Mitzi. "I wonder what they're worth."

"There's a guide here in the back, but it's probably out-of-date by now." She flipped the pages. "For the whole set, it says the most you could get for them is about thirty dollars."

"Thelma only had a couple of them."

"Well, then you probably would only get a few

dollars. People like to buy a complete set. I'm sorry."
She started to close the book.

"When were they made? I'm wondering if all
Thelma's buttons were from the same period."

Mitzi flipped back to where the photo was. "It says
they were sweater buttons produced in the sixties." She stared at them, and I swear she blushed.
"They're—well, they're a little risqué, aren't they?"

I hadn't thought about it.

"Wouldn't the ones that say 'Danger' and 'Proceed
with Caution' be a little suggestive"—she ran her
hand down her ample chest—"sewn down the front
of a cardigan?"

Not as suggestive as some of the things written on
T-shirts today, I thought, and suddenly the buttons
didn't sound like a warning cry from Thelma after all.

Mitzi was staring at the page. "Of course, they
aren't as bad as some of the buttons from the eighteenth century." She'd been talking softly before, but
her voice fell to a whisper. "They were actually por-
nographic. Well-bred women like ourselves didn't
dare look at them."

Speak for yourself, Mitzi, I thought as I got up and
prepared to spy on her neighbors. Maybe I would even
find Deke and Biker Babe or Naomi and Frankie in a
compromising position in the backseat of a one-eyed
car.

Mitzi sniffed delicately and closed the book. "I like
buttons of historical significance."

"I think Genevieve did say that you had a collection
of presidential buttons."

Mitzi gave a little gasp. "I'm surprised Genevieve
said that. She's the one with the big collection."

I glanced at my watch. I was anxious to get away, but after the coffee, I asked if I could use Mitzi's bathroom before I left. I certainly didn't want to start my surveillance and then have to leave for a restroom-run to a service station halfway through the stakeout.

Mitzi was waiting for me with another book when I came out. "Would you like to see a picture of one of my presidential buttons?" The book was open to a page with a turned-down corner. "It's my pride and joy."

The photo showed a small brass button with a log cabin on it. According to a caption below it, a barrel on the front porch held hard liquor.

"The button's a family heirloom," Mitzi said. "My great-great-grandfather knew William Henry Harrison, and this is from his 1840 campaign. It's been handed down from one generation to the next."

The way she said it with such awe made me think she was probably into genealogy, too.

She tapped on the picture. "It was meant to symbolize General Harrison's humble beginnings, but to tell the truth, he didn't drink and he was of wealthy British birth."

I tried to be polite, but I was already late getting to my observation post.

"Earlier presidential buttons were commemoratives," she said. "We didn't have true campaign buttons like this until 1834, and by 1840 polite politics had given way to rough-and-tumble campaigning."

Good, maybe that meant the political buttons I'd inherited from my Uncle Chet were worth something. My favorite said "Democrats Make Better Lovers—We've Been Screwed for Years in Colorado."

Mitzi dashed my hopes immediately, her soft voice rising in disdain. "Of course, after 1896 they started having pins on the back of the buttons, but for the first hundred years, political buttons were true buttons that could be sewn on clothes."

I knew for a fact that political buttons with—God forbid—pins on the back were collectibles in their own right, but I guess not to button purists.

Why was I letting myself get diverted from my next mission? I edged toward the door.

Mitzi followed me. She had turned to another page, and she was showing me a picture of a button that had the initials G.W. on it in a fancy script. "This is a George Washington button from his second inauguration. There are said to be twenty-seven different designs of his inaugural buttons, but this one has the initials of the original thirteen colonies in circles around the border along with the words 'Long Live the President.' Did your friend have one of these, by any chance?"

I shook my head.

"If she did, it could be quite valuable. I know Genevieve's collection is far more extensive than mine, and she'd give almost anything to get her hands on a genuine George Washington button."

"I'm quite sure Thelma didn't have one," I said, and if she had, I would have put Genevieve's name at the top of my suspect list. "Now I must apologize. I really have to leave. Thanks for the cake and coffee. They were great." I was blubbering in my haste to get away.

"Are you sure you wouldn't like some more coffee and another piece of cake?"

I kept shaking my head. "I really have to get going."

"Well, come back again sometime, and if you'll give me more notice, I'll go to the safe-deposit box and get my log cabin button so you can see it."

Mitzi gave me such a sad-eyed look that I almost set up another date with her for the next week.

And she wasn't done yet. "You might be interested to know that Ronald Reagan was the first president since Washington to give buttons as souvenirs at his inauguration. They were lovely blazer buttons."

"Thanks for your help."

"It's nice having company," she said in her little-girl voice as I made my way to my car. Yep, I definitely needed to hook her up with Willetta in the next block.

I drove around the corner and parked south of Naomi's house where I could get a clear view of her driveway as well as Thelma's. Unfortunately, Thelma's car, which I presumed Deke and Leilani were using, and the red-and-white convertible from Naomi and Frankie's driveway were both gone.

On the bright side, both cars would have to return at some point during the evening and then I could see if either car had a burned-out headlight. I locked my doors and got a blanket out of the backseat to keep warm on this crisp October night. Then I hunkered down to wait.

But stakeouts can be boring. I wondered if Mitzi had slipped me some decaf coffee. I felt myself getting drowsy. I tried biting my lower lip and wiggling around in my seat. It didn't work. At some point, I fell asleep.

Fine detective I would be. I know because, all of a sudden, my cell phone rang. I was so startled I banged my hand on the horn in an effort to disentangle myself from the blanket. Talk about making noise. The phone was nothing compared to the blaring of the horn. And where was the stupid phone, anyway?

I finally found it in the bottom of my purse. "Hello," I whispered in a Mitzi-like voice, still not awake enough to realize that, if the honking horn hadn't alerted someone, then my voice wasn't going to.

"Yo, Mandy," Nat said on the other end. "So you actually moved into the new millennium. Knowing you, I figured you'd have the cell phone turned off."

"What do you want?" I sounded grouchy, but my nerves were seriously jangled by then.

"I called about your sweetie."

"About what? Oh, you mean about Frankie?"

"Yeah, about Frankie Panky." He said the name in a silly falsetto voice. "Who'd you think I was talking about?"

"Okay, will you just cut to the chase." When I talked to Nat, I always fell into his cliché-riddled way of speaking. "What did you find out about him?"

"I didn't find out nothin'. Nada. Zippo. Zilch. A big fat zero." Trust Nat to overdo on the negatives. "Your fella doesn't seem to have a criminal record in the state of Colorado. At least, not anything that's been reported in the paper."

A dog came bounding by on the sidewalk, and I could hear a man yelling to stop him. For a minute, I thought the dog was going to find me out. He stopped, sniffed at my car, perhaps mistaking it for a fireplug, and then raced off again, his owner in hot pursuit. I ducked down in my seat as the man went by.

"I thought you'd be happy that Mandy Pandy's Frankie Panky is clean." Again the sappy voice.

The dog began to bark from somewhere up the street.

"Oh, I am," I said, but of course, I really wasn't. I'd been hoping to find out something about Naomi's boyfriend that I could take to the cops. I sure wasn't finding out anything about Thelma's buttons.

"Do I hear a dog?" Nat asked. "Where are you anyway?"

A car drove past, its light sweeping across the interior of my Hyundai. I tried to melt into the upholstery, but the steering wheel got in the way. I had to lean over into the passenger seat. The car sounded as if it were turning into a driveway, and the dog was heading back in my direction.

"I hear a car, and the dog sounds like he's about to attack," Nat yelled. "What the hell are you doing—spying on your boyfriend?"

He was closer to the truth than he realized. I decided to sneak a look out the front window. I didn't see the dog and its owner, but the car had pulled into Naomi's driveway. Its lights were already out. Damn. Naomi was standing by the front passenger door, and Frankie was at the curb, staring in my direction. I ducked down again, praying they hadn't seen me and would go into the house.

A few moments later someone started banging on my window. It matched the pounding of my heart. I'd been found out.

ELEVEN

I SHOULD HAVE SCREAMED for Nat to call the police. In my panic, I punched the off button and hung up on him. I would call the police myself just as soon as I managed to slink down to the floor and hide.

Oh, yeah, like the person outside couldn't see me wedged halfway under the dashboard. But maybe whoever it was would think I'd passed out and would conveniently go away.

"Get away from there." A gruff voice came from somewhere in the distance.

I didn't dare breathe. The banging quit, then came again a few moments later. I started to hit the button to alert the police to my predicament when I heard another voice. "Damn it, Mandy, get out of here."

Frankie didn't know my name, and besides, the voice sounded familiar. I edged up in the seat and peered out into the dark. Mack's face was pressed against the other side of the glass.

I rolled down the window. "What are you doing here?"

"Damn it. No time to talk. Get going. *Now*. I'll meet you at the diner where we ate last night."

I nodded dumbly and started the car. What was Mack doing here? Was it Frankie who'd tried to chase him away? I sped past Naomi's house. Frankie was now back by his car, still looking our way. Naomi was on the front porch. If they hadn't seen me before, they had now.

I slowed as I turned the corner and skidded to a stop. Where was Mack's pickup? I waited for a few seconds, but I felt another stab of fear. What if Mack had been attacked by Frankie and some of his unseen hooligans? I made a quick U-turn and headed back in the direction of Naomi's house.

As I did, I saw Mack turning his truck around in the middle of the street and heading toward me. His vanity license plate, MAC TRK, stuck out like a neon sign. Apparently, he'd been parked across the street; we were now going in opposite directions again. Mack noticed me and did another U-turn, completing a full circle by bouncing over the curb in front of the house across from Thelma's.

We still had the rapt attention of Frankie and Naomi, plus the dog and his owner, who was trying to restrain the barking animal as it lunged at my car. Nothing like calling attention to ourselves big time.

I made a right turn at the next corner, then a left and a right again until I reached Seventeenth, which would eventually turn into a one-way street heading downtown. Mack stayed on my back bumper all the way. I just hoped Frankie wasn't following him in a car that, despite all my efforts to find out, might or might not have a burned-out headlight.

Mack would doubtless chew me out as soon as we got to the diner, but I could do the same thing to him. He'd probably been keeping an eye on me and had ducked down, too, when all the noise started.

I glanced at my watch. Good grief. It was already eleven o'clock. I wondered how long I'd slept.

I pulled into a parking space at the diner and got out of the car to wait for Mack. He swung into the space next to me, jumped down, and hustled me inside the restaurant.

"Do you think they followed us here?" I asked, mainly because of the grip he had on my elbow.

"I don't think so."

A waitress approached us once we got inside. She took us to a booth and asked us if we knew what we wanted. We both said we'd take cheeseburgers and coffee, which was the same thing we'd had the night before.

As soon as that was dispensed with, I started on the offensive. "So what were you doing following me?" I tried to look indignant. "I'm an adult. I can take care of myself."

"Sure you can." Mack shook his head as if he'd given up on me long ago. "You had no business going out there if someone had already spotted your car."

"But you shouldn't have followed me."

"Dang, I wasn't following you."

So how had he known where to find me? I started to say something, but I realized it would have been easy enough for Mack to look up Thelma's address on our computer at work.

"I figured nobody would know my truck," he said, "so I decided to swing by there after rehearsal and look around for a one-eyed car. I'd no sooner pulled up to the curb than I saw you parked across the street."

"I was that obvious, huh?"

"To tell the truth, I didn't notice you at first. Then all of a sudden this horn started blaring, and I thought it was someone's car alarm going off. About that time, a car came around the corner and lit up the Hyundai. That's when I realized it was you. What the hell were you trying to do—raise the dead?"

"If you must know, I fell asleep. Then all of a sudden my cell phone started ringing, and I was trying to find it."

"I told you all these new-fangled contraptions would get you in more trouble than they're worth."

I was beginning to agree. After all, it was the phone's going off the previous night that had called Mack's attention to my late arrival at the theater. Maybe I was going to have to abandon it if I wanted to remain inconspicuous.

I still wasn't ready to admit that to Mack. "But it was probably you running over to the car that attracted people's attention."

"No way. The man who pulled into the driveway— I presume it was this Frankie guy you were telling me about—got out and came over to your car. As soon as I jumped out of my truck and yelled at him, he backed off."

So that had been Mack using one of his scary stage voices. I dropped my head. "Okay, I guess I owe you an apology, but we still haven't found the one-eyed car."

When I looked back up, Mack was grinning. "Never fear. Some of us are always alert and vigilant. The convertible that pulled into the driveway had a burned-out headlight."

"You're kidding." I wanted to give him a hug, but

it was too far to reach across the table. "So it was Frank Pankovich who was following me."

Mack nodded. "Looks that way."

"So that's how you knew he didn't follow us."

"Yep, so aren't you glad I was there?" The waitress returned with our coffee, and Mack waited until she left. "Now you need to take your suspicions to the police and be done with it."

If only Nat had found out something incriminating about Frank Pankovich...I was afraid the police would blow off my concerns and cite me for harassment or, even worse, stalking. At least that's what I might do in similar circumstances.

I filled Mack in on my visit to Mitzi Porter's while we waited for the burgers and later while we ate them. However, I left out the part about the discovery of the buttons that said "Danger" and "Proceed with Caution." That would only set him off again, and he didn't need any reminders to do that.

At my car, he said, "Don't forget to pay the two dollars." I knew, of course, that he was referring to Cary Grant's adventures with the police in *North by Northwest*.

Apparently, the phrase was going to become his code words to warn me to stay out of trouble in the future. He didn't need to bother. The whole experience that night had unnerved me.

I slept fitfully. After tossing and turning for what seemed like hours, I finally got up and wrote the check for the speeding ticket I'd gotten when I was being pursued by the one-eyed car the night before. In my exhausted state, I was hoping it would get me in the good graces of the cops when I went to them with my story about Frankie.

There was one final thing I wanted to do before I called them. I got out the phone book and let my fingers wander through the yellow pages—about the only physical activity I was capable of that time of night. Finally I found private investigators under the *I*'s, not the *P*'s.

If Nat couldn't find out anything about Frank Pankovich, maybe a detective could. My gut told me that Frankie was hiding something, and I needed to find out what it was before he tracked me down. Besides, I would be up-front this time about why I wanted to know. No feigning a romantic interest in the guy the way I had with Nat. And while I was at it, I would have the investigator look up Deke, Leilani, and Naomi as well.

My fingers stopped on the first P.I. in the book. AAA Investigations. Triple A. Maybe it had the seal of approval of the car folks, but I doubted it. The main thing it had going for it was that it was on Broadway, not far from my apartment. I would stop there on my way to work the next morning since it was Mack's week to open up the plant. With that decision made, I finally was able to go back to sleep.

THE OFFICE WAS on the tenth floor of a high rise. Somehow I'd imagined that it would be in a run-down building with no elevator. I was sure Thelma's favorite detective, Sam Spade, never had an office like this.

When I opened the door, a middle-aged receptionist asked if I had an appointment. It took me off guard.

"I guess I should have called ahead," I said. It had

never occurred to me that a private eye wouldn't take walk-ins, but maybe I'd read too many of Thelma's paperbacks.

"It probably would have been advisable, but I'll see if we can fit you in." She gave me a kindly smile. Definitely not the type of secretary Mike Hammer would have had, but perhaps I should forget the stereotypes. "If you'll give me your name and tell me what you want, I'll see if Trav—Mr. Kincaid—is free right now."

It was the name that totally distracted me. I'd known a Travis Kincaid once, but no, it couldn't be him. He was probably in prison by now.

"I, well, uh—" I was wondering if I should turn around and leave, just in case it was him.

The receptionist looked sympathetic. "I probably should tell you that we don't handle divorce cases." Apparently she thought I was too embarrassed to tell her that I wanted to hire someone to tail a philandering husband.

"No, it isn't that."

She seemed relieved. "Then give me your name and I'll ask Mr. Kincaid if he can see you."

I rummaged around in my mind for an alias. I was sure the Travis I remembered wouldn't remember me. After all, it had been nearly twenty years. Still, it was possible he'd remember my name. So what was the name I'd given to Willetta? Unable to think of it, I finally gave up. "I'm Ms. Dyer, and I wanted to see if someone here could run a background check for me."

She picked up the phone, said a few words, and escorted me to the door of an inner office.

When I got inside, all I could see was the back of a man's head. His dark hair, which curled around the top of his shirt collar, had a few gray strands beginning to show in it. He had his feet on a window ledge and appeared to be going through some computer printouts.

The feet on the ledge fit my outdated image of a private eye; the computer printouts did not.

He dropped his feet and swung around in his chair. "What can I do for you, Ms. Dyer?"

He was the image of Sam Spade and Mike Hammer, all rolled into one. Good-looking in a slightly disheveled way, his tie loosened at the neck, and a cynical expression on his face as if he'd seen and heard it all.

Worse yet, I did know him. He'd been the loner on a motorcycle back in high school, a senior teetering on the brink of expulsion when I was a sophomore. Somehow he'd managed to graduate, never to be seen or heard from again. Until now.

He'd looked older than he really was back in school, but his age had finally caught up to his dark, swarthy features. He hadn't changed at all.

Since he obviously wasn't in jail, as I'd have predicted, my next guess would have been that he was a member of Hell's Angels, riding with the likes of Deke Wolfe. When I thought about it some more, a private eye was not beyond the realm of possibility. However, I would have figured him for the type who *did* handle divorce cases, the raunchier the better.

He was looking at me as if he was trying to place me, and I considered my options. I could say I'd made a mistake and get out of the office before he recognized me, or I could state my business like the mature, self-assured businesswoman I'd become.

He continued to look me up and down with what some people called bedroom eyes—dark and piercing as though he had X-ray vision. It wasn't that he scared me; he just made me nervous. Always had, always would.

"Okay." I moved my own eyes to the view of the downtown high-rises outside his window. It was sure a lot better view than I had from my office. I took a deep breath and tried to pull myself together. "I wanted to see if you could run a background check for me on some people. Their names are—"

"Why?"

"Excuse me?" I knew what he'd said, and I'd planned to tell him the whole story. That's when I'd expected that the private investigator would be a total stranger with whom I would have a brief professional relationship. But did I want to tell Travis Kincaid, the tough kid from our neighborhood, all the things I'd refused to tell my good friend Nat?

"Why do you want to know?" he repeated.

I looked over at him. His eyes were boring into me, but at least he was no longer looking below the neck. "Does a private investigator have the same relationship with a client that an attorney does?" I asked finally.

"I can assure you I'll treat the matter with complete confidentiality." He smiled as if he was trying to reassure me, but it made me notice the white sliver of a scar at the edge of his rather sensual lips. Nat had always thought he'd received it in a knife fight with someone who'd crossed him.

Still, he no longer seemed to be trying to figure out where he'd met me. My story wasn't incriminating or anything, and the information I wanted shouldn't be that difficult for him to find. We could handle it over the telephone, and that would be the end of it.

Finally, I made up my mind. I laid out my suspicions about Thelma's death. Before I went to the police, I explained, I wanted to check out four of her acquaintances to see if they might bear further investigation as suspects in her death.

He wrote notes, no longer giving me the penetrating where-have-I-met-her-before looks when he glanced up. He asked me how to spell the names Dexter Wolfe, Frank Pankovich, and their respective girlfriends.

"I'm not positive about how to spell Frank's last name," I said.

"No problem. I'll try several spellings and get back to you. Want to give me a number where I can reach you?"

Now that he hadn't recognized me, I was feeling a little better. It was probably stupid, anyway, to think that he would remember me just because Nat and I remembered him. I gave him my phone numbers, both at home and work.

"Thanks," I said, getting up to leave.

"Don't you want to know how much I charge?" he asked.

Nope, what I wanted to do was get out of there.

"Sure," I said.

He handed me a contract to look at and sign. "We charge one hundred dollars an hour. The kind of information you want shouldn't take more than an hour or two."

"Fine." I signed my name as illegibly as possible—Amanda Dyer. I used my full given name just in case seeing the name Mandy in black and white might trigger some latent memory of where he'd known me before.

I handed the contract to him and started for the door.

"By the way," he said just as I had my hand on the doorknob, "you never did tell me why you stood me up in high school."

TWELVE

DAMN, DAMN, DAMN. He'd known who I was the whole time. He'd been toying with me just the way he did with kids back in school.

I pretended that I didn't hear him as I hurried out to the reception area.

The motherly-looking woman was still at her desk. She glanced at me and smiled. "Was Mr. Kincaid able to help you?"

"I don't know." It was a stupid reply, but I was intent on escape.

As soon as I reached the street, my first thought was that I had to tell Nat. This was too weird to keep to myself. I started over to the *Tribune* office, on the outskirts of the downtown area, hoping he'd be at his desk. If Nat had ever run into our high school nemesis himself, I was sure he would have broken a few speed records to give me a news bulletin about it.

I stopped midway across Broadway. I couldn't go to Nat, not unless I was prepared to tell him the whole story of why I'd hired a private investigator in the first place. I wasn't yet ready to explain the real reason I wanted to find out about Frank Pankovich. On the other hand, I didn't think Nat would buy the story that I'd sicced a P.I. on my newfound lover.

I did a quick about-face in the middle of the intersection and barely made it back to my original side of the street before the light changed. In lieu of telling Nat, I unloaded on Mack as soon as I got to work. Unfortunately, I didn't realize he'd find the story amusing.

"You'll be glad to know," I said, seeking him out in his usual place in the dry-cleaning department, "that I've put the whole thing in the hands of a private investigator. He's going to run background checks on Frank Pankovich and Deke Wolfe and their girlfriends to see if any of them have something to hide."

"Now you're finally getting smart," Mack said. He removed a load of dark clothes from the larger of our two cleaning machines and started separating the pants from the other garments in the load. I joined him in laying the pants over a laundry cart. That way they'd be easier for our pants presser to grab when he was ready for them.

"Only trouble is the investigator turned out to be someone Nat and I knew from school," I said. "He wasn't a person you wanted to tangle with."

Mack continued separating out the garments. "How so?"

"He was really wild."

"And just how did that affect you?" He stopped what he was doing and gave me his worried parental look. He was always concerned about any missteps I might have taken from birth to the present.

I stuttered a little because, of course, it didn't affect me. Not unless you counted the date that never happened, and I wasn't about to tell Mack about that.

"Well, he was always picking on the smaller kids." I didn't add that my information came secondhand from Nat. I'd always suspected that Nat, the pip-squeak, had been on the short end of Travis's taunting back in grade school. That was before I even moved into the neighborhood.

All of a sudden Mack grinned.

"What?" I asked.

"You mean you and Nat were among his 'nameless rabble of victims.'"

"What're you talking about?"

"Don't you remember the line from *A Christmas Story:* 'In our world, you were either a bully, a toadie, or one of the nameless rabble of victims'?" Mack looked pleased with himself for squeezing a movie quote into the conversation. "It's from the film about the boy who wanted a Red Ryder air rifle for Christmas."

"I know what it's from," I said.

And if he wasn't going to take my conversation seriously, see if I would ever tell him anything again. For that matter, I wasn't even going to help him with the load of clothes. I turned and continued to the front of the plant.

"Maybe he changed," Mack yelled after me.

But I kept thinking about Nat and me as "the nameless rabble of victims." That's what we'd been, all right. I refused to be part of the rabble anymore or to let Travis unnerve me now that we were all grown up.

If he mentioned anything about the date when he called me with the information about Frankie and company, I'd think up some mature-sounding response. However, it certainly wouldn't be the mealy-mouthed truth: Nat had talked me out of going on the date because he'd convinced me that Travis would either seduce me or make me be a lookout when he robbed a gas station.

At the time, I'd failed to see the logic that neither of these events was likely to occur on the back of a motorcycle. In fact, one of the things I'd long suspected was that Nat, who frequently rode around on a motorcycle himself these days, did so because he was trying to emulate the tough-guy image of his childhood nemesis/hero, Travis Kincaid.

Enough wallowing in the rabble of the past.

Once I found out that my counter people had everything under control up front, I headed back to my office. I was getting way behind in my paperwork because of the diversions of the last few days. Now that I was more convinced than ever that Frank Pankovich of the one-eyed car had something to do with Thelma's death, finding out about the buttons no longer seemed a priority.

Mack hailed me from his spotting board, where he'd gone back to prespotting another load of clothes to be cleaned. "By the way, Harvest phoned this morning and said Genevieve wanted to know where you worked."

I came to a stop. "What did you tell her?"

"Well, I told her you worked here, of course."

Mack obviously didn't have the same suspicious nature that I did. Maybe I should have had Travis do a background check on Genevieve as well, even if she was a member of the country club set, and maybe I should keep checking on those buttons, after all.

First to the paperwork, which of course was a misnomer since I handled it all on the computer. I had no sooner sat down at my desk than I heard a banging on my office door.

"Who is it?"

"It's me—Betty."

I sighed. "I'll be out in a few minutes."

"No, it ain't that. I got somebody here to see you."

I could almost guarantee that it was someone I didn't want to see, probably Les the Rag Man.

Before I had a chance to answer, Betty yelled, "It's Les."

I was right. Betty opened the door and stepped aside to let Les enter the room. "Remember how I said he could probably help you? He made a special trip down here just to look at the buttons."

Like Mitzi's coconut cake the night before, it was hard to refuse Les after he'd gone to all that trouble.

The pencil-thin ragman came into the room in mismatched clothes that were as eclectic as the buttons he sold me on his periodic visits to the cleaners. He had on a pair of woolen dress slacks, a plaid flannel shirt, a Denver Broncos jacket with a long-discarded logo on it, and a pair of scruffy Reeboks. He whisked off a black beret, revealing a graying cowlick that made a tuft of hair on the crown of his head stand at attention. I would have bet he was in his late fifties, but the cowlick and his prominent Adam's apple made him look like a wizened teenager.

"Hello, Miss Mandy," he said. "Betty here says you got some buttons she's sure got diamonds and rubies in 'em and that you wanted me to take a look at them." With that, he held up what, I swear, looked like a jeweler's loupe.

"Where'd you get that?" I asked.

He shrugged. "I used to work in a jewelry store."

"Well, duh," Betty said. "Why'd you think I asked him to come down here and help you out?"

"I was a watchmaker until I got squeezed out of the business by all those dadburned battery-operated digital watches," he said.

I wasn't ready to give him my seal of approval as an expert yet. "But what does that have to do with precious gems?"

"Never you fear. I learned a thing or two about the jewelry business while I was there. In fact, I've found some pretty interesting stones masquerading as costume jewelry since I been in my current business."

Okay, so what did I have to lose? I showed him the pile of dresses on the sofa and told him to have at it. "Thanks, Betty, for showing him in," I said to his self-appointed business manager. "You can go back to work now."

"But I want to watch."

Les pushed my only guest chair over next to the clothes, put the loupe's attached band over his head, adjusted the eyepiece, and set to work.

Betty leaned over him. "This one's cute, ain't it?" She'd zeroed in on a Mickey Mouse button.

"I said you can go now, Betty." I quickly moved my chair from the desk to oversee the project.

Les tapped a finger on Mickey. "You may be right. This could be worth a lot more than some of the others, at least to a Disney collector."

Betty gave me a smug look, and I pointed her to the door. "Go."

"Okay, I'm goin', but you don't have to get your drawers all twisted up in a knot about it."

I pointed to a button with a large diamondlike stone in it. "How about this one?"

Les closed one eye to peer at it. "Nope," he said. "It's too perfect, but there's something called a diamond tester you can buy. A diamond'll conduct heat back to the tester and make it beep. Glass won't."

Betty stopped. "You ought to get one of those testers, boss lady."

"Out, Betty."

"I said I was goin'."

She had reached the door when Ann Marie from the front counter showed up, and they almost collided.

"Teenagers!" Betty said as if that explained everything. "You like to have knocked me down, girl." With that, she finally made her exit.

"There's someone out at the counter who wants to see you," Ann Marie said. "What'll I do with her?"

I was getting seriously irritated with all the interruptions. "What does she want?"

Ann Marie looked confused. "I didn't ask."

"Did she give her name?"

Ann Marie nodded.

"And?"

"I couldn't really catch it."

"What's your best guess?"

"It sounded like 'Misty' or something." She gave it Mitzi's little-girl inflection.

I didn't want to leave Les alone with the buttons in case he found the Hope Diamond hiding in one of them. "Okay, send her back here, will you?"

"Okeydoke," Ann Marie said. She gave a little pirouette and left.

Les continued to scrutinize the buttons, rejecting one after the other. "Nope, sorry, just paste."

It took a while for Mitzi to arrive, but I heard her tread outside the door before I actually saw her. Or maybe it was Ann Marie skipping along ahead of her.

"Here's Miss Dyer." Ann Marie gave a little flourish of her hand toward me as she entered the room a step ahead of the heavyset button collector.

"You poor little thing," Mitzi said to me in her girlish voice. "The more we got to talking about it, the more we realized we should offer to help you identify the buttons in your collection."

"Who's we?"

"Oh, Genevieve, of course. She called and gave me your address because she thought it was a good idea if I would offer my assistance."

Genevieve again. I wondered if she'd sent Mitzi as her scout before she came in person with an offer to take the buttons off my hands. But from what Les was telling me, the buttons might not be worth enough to be a motive for murder or anything else.

"Join the crowd," I said finally.

"Okeydoke," Ann Marie said, always eager to get out of work.

"Not you, Ann Marie."

"Okeydoke." With a toss of her ponytail, she left.

"This is Les." He barely glanced around. "And this is Mitzi. When you get through looking at the buttons, why don't you hand the dresses to her? She wants to see if any of them would be valuable to button collectors."

Mitzi sat in my desk chair and whipped out a magnifying glass as if she were Sherlock Holmes in drag.

Ever the matchmaker, I wondered if I could get the lonely Mitzi hooked up with Les, since they both obviously had an interest in buttons. However, since I'd never been notably successful in this sideline, I decided it probably wasn't worth my effort.

"Hmmm," Mitzi said. "I didn't realize they were sewn on dresses. What a peculiar way to store a collection."

"Buttons on dresses," Les said. "Who'd'a ever thunk?"

"Hmmph," Mitzi said indignantly, but with her soft voice it sounded a lot like her previous "Hmmm."

Les was looking at a row of glittering diamondlike buttons on a yellow-and-orange floral shirtwaist. They caught the light as he twisted them back and forth.

"All glass," he said finally, handing them to Mitzi.

"Not many diamonds have been used in buttons since the eighteenth century," she said. "These are rhinestones."

He gave her a dirty look. "That's what I said. Rhinestones are nothin' but paste or glass with a foil backing to make 'em reflect the light."

She ignored him. "They're probably from the thirties. Rhinestone became very popular during the Depression. We call the paste ones imitation rhinestones."

She took the dresses as Les handed them to her and stopped at the army button I'd noticed earlier. "Some people collect uniform buttons," she said, "but I don't know much about them. Of course, this one looks like it's from World War I or II so it probably wouldn't be worth much. What people like to collect are earlier buttons from the Civil War or off railroad uniforms. That sort of thing.''

Mitzi put the dress aside and grabbed another one from the pile that Les had discarded. ''Now this is more like it.'' She tapped a red-and-white button with a geometric design. ''This could be made of Bakelite, which was invented in 1909 and was the first all-synthetic plastic.''

Les whipped through the rest of the dresses quickly. There weren't that many jeweled buttons among them. ''I'd say you might as well just add these to the ones you buy from me,'' he said, getting up to leave.

Mitzi gave us a curious look.

''I have a lot of buttons we use for replacements on customers' clothes,'' I explained.

''Oh.''

I handed Les a twenty-dollar tip for his efforts, although he probably would have preferred to think of it as remuneration for a professional appraisal.

He smiled, put on his beret, and disappeared.

Mitzi turned her attention to a black button with a carved head on it that looked as if were inspired by a statue on Easter Island. ''This could be Bakelite, too,'' she said. ''Genevieve collects Bakelite jewelry as well as presidential buttons, and she might be interested in buying this. Bakelite's heavier than other plastics, but one of the best ways to tell is to give it a hot needle test. The needle will go into other plastics, but it won't go into Bakelite. Another way—''

Suddenly someone yelled from out in the plant, ''Emergency in the laundry. Hey, boss lady, we got an emergency.'' One guess who it was.

I glanced at Mitzi, who was already engrossed in

studying another button with her magnifying glass. I took off at a run. Mack was already at the washers by the time I got there.

Betty looked at us and shrugged. "Never mind. I thought for a minute we got too much soap in the machine, but I think everything's okay after all."

Since the chemicals were administered automatically, I was sure it was.

"So how about the buttons?" Betty asked. "Did Les find any diamonds and rubies?"

"Not a one." I whipped around and returned to my office, sure that was the only reason for the "emergency." I would have liked to apply a red-hot needle to her if I'd had one handy.

Mitzi jumped as I entered the room. "Oh, mercy, I didn't hear you come back. You scared me to death."

I wondered if I'd really scared her or if her reaction was a guilty response to something she'd been doing that she didn't want me to see.

She stood up. "Well, I'm afraid that's it. I'd say the whole collection might be worth five hundred to a thousand dollars. That's a rough estimate, of course, but it would make a nice start for you in case you ever wanted to get into button collecting."

"Thanks, but I don't have much time for hobbies." Not unless one considered my sideline of looking for clues to a murder that no one else believed had happened. For all I knew, Frankie and Naomi had followed me Monday night simply because they wondered what I was up to.

All the same, I checked the buttons after Mitzi left to see if she'd taken any of them in the few moments I'd been out of the office. It was hard to tell, but I didn't think so. At least the Bakelite buttons were still there.

I was depressed that the buttons apparently weren't worth a lot of money. I might have to give up the whole idea that Thelma had been murdered unless Travis Kincaid discovered something suspicious about Frank Pankovich. I waited for his call. I just didn't expect him to show up in person shortly before closing time.

THIRTEEN

I WAS ALREADY IN a funk by the time Theresa, my afternoon counter manager, told me a Mr. Kincaid was waiting for me at the front counter.

Betty had been bugging me all afternoon about hopping in my car—with her along, of course—and going to Boulder to see if her friend Buttons the ventriloquist could help about the buttons. Forty miles to Boulder in rush-hour traffic. No thanks.

"Well, if that's the way you want to be about it," she'd said and stomped off once her shift was over.

Now I had to face Travis in person, but at least I was hopeful he would have some information that would allow me to dump the whole matter in the hands of the police. Like a mantra, I kept repeating "I refuse to be part of the rabble" as I made my way through the plant.

"So what did you find out?" I asked as soon as I reached the counter.

Travis was wearing a brown tweed sports jacket over his brown slacks, and his tie was now in place, not askew the way it had been this morning. He no longer exuded the tough-guy image—except when he smiled. Then I could see the white scar at the corner of his lip.

"I found out some interesting things," he said,

glancing around at the half dozen customers and my two counter people. "I'd rather not talk about them here. Maybe we could discuss them over dinner."

Nope, I wasn't getting sucked into that. I glanced at my watch. It was after six o'clock. "I'm sorry, I have to be here to close up at seven. Why don't we—"

"I can wait," he said.

I'd been about to suggest that we go into the fitting room at the far end of the call office.

"That's all right, Mandy," Theresa said, always the helpful employee. "I can close for you. Why don't you go on out for dinner? You never have any fun anymore."

I would have liked to throttle her, but I didn't even give her a dirty look. I didn't dare, or Travis would be sure to notice it with those piercing dark eyes of his. Then he would lift his left eyebrow in that skeptical, intimidating way he used to do in school.

"All right," I said. "There's a restaurant called Tico Taco's just behind the cleaners. I'll meet you there in fifteen minutes."

"Good, see you then." He left and went around the side of the building.

I returned to my office to get my coat and shoulder bag. I didn't even change out of my tan-and-yellow slacks-and-blouse uniform. The better to convey that I saw this dinner as the business meeting it was, not a fun day of playing hooky.

I did a few deep-breathing exercises for ten minutes, then set out across the parking lot for the strip shopping center behind the plant. I was glad Mack had already left for the day. He would have been sure to kid me about meeting with one of "the bullies and toadies" if he'd known where I was going.

Manuel Ramirez, the owner of Tico Taco's, came up to me the moment I entered the restaurant. "*Buenas noches,* Mandy." He looked sad, the way he always did when I came in by myself. "You dining alone tonight?"

"No, I was meeting someone here." I glanced around the restaurant, but I couldn't see Travis.

Manuel's eyes lit up. "Oh, you mean the gentleman in the back. He requested a secluded spot." Ever the romantic, the owner winked at me as he led me to the booth.

I probably should have thought twice about meeting the investigator here. Tico Taco's had the advantage of being near the cleaners and my car, but Manuel was apt to overdo on the attention when he thought I was on a date.

"Hi," I said as I slid into the seat opposite Travis, who was facing away from the door.

The restaurant always had tablecloths and candles at night, and Manuel started to make a big production out of lighting our candle.

"You don't need to do that." I put my hand over the candlestick to stop him and almost got burned for my effort.

"Dinner is always better by candlelight," he said, lighting the wick with a flourish of his lighter. "May I suggest a margarita before dinner."

"Sure," Travis said.

I thought about ordering a Virgin Mary, but I didn't want to give my dining companion an opportunity for any smart remarks. "I'll just take iced tea. I have to go back to work when we're through."

Manuel looked crestfallen as he left the booth.

"So what did you find out?" I asked.

"Here's the report on Frank Pankovich." Travis flipped it around toward me. "Seems he's a small-time crook with a record back in Illinois. Is this your guy?" Somehow, Travis had managed to get a mug shot of Frankie, and he handed it to me. It was definitely Thelma's neighbor. "He has several aliases and a long record for burglary with a couple of blackmail schemes thrown in."

My heart did a little tap dance. I'd been right about Frankie. Naomi's sleazy boyfriend could have been in the act of searching Thelma's house when she surprised him and he pushed her down the steps. After all, he could have used Naomi's key to get inside.

"Thanks," I said, trying hard not to seem too grateful. "What about Deke Wolfe?"

Travis handed me another sheet of paper. "He's a legitimate businessman out in California."

I was surprised but relieved to hear that Thelma's nephew wasn't the shady character I'd envisioned.

"He owns a couple of bars, but"—Travis paused for just a beat—"he's in debt way over his head. Apparently, Wolfe has a habit of going up to Vegas on his days off, and the boys up there don't look favorably at the tab he's been running up."

That meant Deke could have been desperate for money. He could have killed his aunt, hoping to inherit enough to pay off his debts.

"How did you find all this information?" I was actually impressed.

He shrugged. "Trade secret. Incidentally, neither of the girlfriends has a record that I could find."

Not unless one considered that they were hanging out with the wrong guys. Just like me.

Manuel returned with our drinks. "And chips and salsa for the lady and her gentleman. They're on the house." He swept them onto the table with an exaggerated gesture of goodwill, and I was relieved that the mariachi band that played on weekends wasn't here. He probably would have sent it over to the table to serenade us. "Do you want to place your dinner order now?"

Travis nodded his head.

I shook mine. "Maybe we'll just have drinks. I really need to get back to work to help close up."

Actually, what I planned to do was phone Stan Foster as soon as I got back to my office. He probably wouldn't be at the police building now, but one of the advantages of having once dated him was that I knew where he lived and how to get in touch with him. I didn't care if he was dating someone else these days. This took priority.

"I'll have the chicken fajitas," Travis said. "Why don't you have some, too? They're on me."

"Fajitas for two," Manuel said. He nodded approvingly, not giving me time to respond before he left.

Why fight it? I hadn't eaten since a quick breakfast on my way to Triple A Investigations this morning. "Okay, but I'm buying."

Travis shrugged again. "Fine, if that's the only way you'll have dinner with me."

I'm sure I turned red in the face from irritation, but he probably interpreted it as blushing. I fumbled in my purse for my checkbook. "How much do I owe you for the work you did?"

"We'll send you a bill. When you see it, you'll wish you'd have let me buy."

I took my hand out of my purse and took a drink of the iced tea. So what did we say now?

"How'd you get to be a P.I.?" I asked.

Travis was squinting at me. "Guess I've always wanted to help people." Yeah, right. "If I remember correctly, I came to your rescue once when you took a header off your bicycle."

That was not something I wanted to talk about. I'd been fifteen at the time, and Nat had let me try out his brand-new Schwinn, a sleek racing model with tires so thin that the slightest rock could send the rider head over tail into a ditch. At least, that's what had happened to me.

I'd cut my cheek, hurt my leg, torn the knee out of my jeans, and badly mangled the bicycle, which had landed on top of me. I kept thinking that Nat was going to kill me when he saw the bike. Then along came Travis and one of his girlfriends on his motorcycle. My humiliation was worse than my wounds.

Travis pulled the bicycle off me, checked to see that I didn't have any broken bones, and then bent the wheel back into a semblance of its proper shape so that I and Nat's bicycle could wobble our way home. What had really scorched my pride was that Travis's girlfriend had insisted that they follow me back to Nat's house. Actually, they didn't follow me. They would roar ahead, then skid to a halt and wait for me, as I made my ignominious way back to Nat's.

"You were pretty banged up," he said. "Did you ever get so you could ride a bike?"

Yep, and I had even mastered the art of stimulating conversation under the right circumstances. Unfortunately, this wasn't one of them. Manuel returned right then with our fajitas and saved me the trouble. Chicken, tomatoes, green pepper, and onions sizzled in an iron skillet.

"An order for two," Manuel said as if our shared meal somehow signaled the start of a steamy new romance. "The pan's hot, so be careful." He transferred the accoutrements—sour cream, guacamole, and salsa—to the table from a tray. "Enjoy." He gave me a sly wink and left.

If that wasn't bad enough, things were about to get even worse. I looked up as our overly sentimental host left, and there was Nat making his way toward me.

I started to put down my iced tea and knocked over the candle. Melted wax spilled across the tablecloth.

"Mandy, where the devil were you last night?" Nat said as he watched me struggle to right the candle. "I tried calling you back on your cell phone, but you didn't answer. Then I left messages, but you never returned my calls."

He must have noticed that someone was sitting across from me, but he probably assumed it was Mack. He started to slip into my side of the booth. When he finally looked across the table, one would have thought he was a student in an acting class asked to convey a whole series of emotions through facial expression: puzzlement at where he'd seen my dinner companion before, stunned recognition, leftover intimidation from childhood, confusion, and then out-and-out irritation.

"I'm not interrupting something, am I?" he asked. "Theresa over at the cleaners told me you were here. I figured you'd be alone. So what the hell is going on?"

"It's okay, Nat." I tried to calm him down, but it was kind of fun to see the grown-up Nat lose his cool. "Do you remember Travis Kincaid from high school? Travis, this is Nat Wilcox."

Travis nodded, obviously recalling one of his rabble of victims. "I see your byline in the *Trib*. How're you doing these days?" He reached out to shake Nat's hand, but Nat was busy giving me a scalding look as if I'd somehow betrayed him the way I had when I returned with the battered bicycle.

Then suddenly he went into a protective mode, something I didn't see much from my longtime buddy. He slid over closer to me. There wasn't anything that was going to blast him out of the booth. And finally, his reporter's curiosity won out over all his other emotions.

"So what"—he motioned between me and Travis—"are the two of you doing here?"

I waited to see what Travis's explanation would be, but he didn't say anything. Silence must be in the investigator's code of honor about client confidentiality.

I thought about telling Nat the truth now that I was a step away from going to the police. However, I didn't want to do it in front of Travis, not after I'd implied to Nat that Frank Pankovich was my current lover.

Nat was waiting impatiently for an answer.

"Uh—Travis came into the cleaners today," I said finally, "and we decided to go out for dinner to catch up on old times." Well, that was certainly the dumbest thing I could have come up with. There were no "old times"—if one ignored the bicycle incident and the date that never happened.

Nat looked over into my lap, where I was discreetly scratching my hands, a sure sign to him that I was lying.

"So what do you do, Travis?" Nat asked.

I guess Travis was following my lead about the real purpose of our dinner meeting. "Oh, this and that," he said noncommittally as he built a fajita for himself.

"Where've you been all these years?" Nat asked.

"Oh, here and there." I could tell Travis was getting a kick out of this.

Manuel came racing back over to the table when he spied Nat. "Are you planning to stay or did you just drop by for a minute to talk to Mandy?" He put the emphasis on the latter possibility, making it apparent that he thought three was a crowd.

"I'll take a beer," Nat said.

"Why don't you have one of our fajitas, Nat?" Travis asked. "There's enough here for all of us."

I wasn't too keen on that idea. Manuel looked downright appalled, as if the idea of fajitas for three was somewhat akin to a menage a trois, but he turned and went to fetch Nat's beer.

I began to create my own fajita, but Nat continued to pepper his old nemesis with questions. All were met with evasive answers.

Frustration was building on Nat's face, but he finally gave up when Manuel returned with his beer.

"Will that be all?" Manuel asked.

Nat nodded and gulped the beer, then grabbed a flour tortilla and piled it high with the fajita fixings.

Mercifully, we ate in comparative silence, and I was relieved when the meal was finally over.

I offered to launder the wax-covered tablecloth for free when Manuel brought the check. He shook his head. I got out my credit card to pay the bill. Manuel shook his head even harder when he took it, undoubtedly being of the old school that believed a gentleman should always pick up the tab.

From Nat's disgusted look, I gathered that he concurred, but I knew from personal experience that it was a crock. Nat loved for me to buy.

When we got outside the restaurant, it was a toss-up which one of my companions could outlast the other.

Travis finally broke away. "Thanks for the dinner."

"You still ride a motorcycle?" Nat asked.

Travis grinned, but I like to think he didn't know that Nat's Harley was probably out in front of the cleaners. "No, I outgrew that years ago. Good seeing you both again." He turned and walked around to the front of the cleaners, where I presumed his car was parked.

Nat's face turned red, but he definitely wasn't blushing. As soon as Travis disappeared around the corner of the building, he let out a whoosh of air. "Well, I never would have believed it if I didn't see it with my own eyes."

"Look, let's go back—" I'd been planning to suggest that we go inside the cleaners so I could tell him the whole story about Frankie.

Nat wouldn't let me finish. "So how long have you been dating Travis?" He spit out the name as if it were a dirty word. "And when were you planning to tell me?"

I was dumbstruck. It had never occurred to me that he would put that particular spin on the dinner.

"And while we're at it, what about Frankie Panky?" This time Nat used the same silly inflection he'd used before when he said the name. "The poor bastard. I find out he's clean as the driven snow, and now you're two-timing him with the guy who was voted 'most likely to go into a life of crime' in high school."

I couldn't resist. "It's *pure* as the driven snow," I said.

"Who the hell cares?"

"And besides, we didn't have a category like that back in high school."

Nat was really on a rip now. "You always did have the hots for Travis, didn't you?"

"Oh, quit being such a jerk, Nat."

He didn't answer. He headed around the corner of the cleaners, presumably to mount his Harley, but not with the same macho pride he usually had.

FOURTEEN

FENCE-MENDING WAS in order, but I would have to wait until Nat cooled off and I got over being angry at him.

In my wildest imagination, I would never have expected Nat to interpret my lie as having to do with a clandestine affair with his dreaded enemy, Travis Kincaid. Go figure.

I glanced at my watch. It was a quarter to eight. All of the employees were gone, the light was on above the back door of the cleaners, and Theresa had indeed locked up the building.

I let myself in the door, punched in the numbers on our security system to deactivate our alarm, then reset it and continued to my office. When I reached my phone, I dialed the home number for Stan Foster.

A woman answered. I couldn't help thinking of the warning: If a woman answers—or was it a man?—hang up. I almost did, but damn it, this was strictly business. So what if the call was from a former girlfriend?

"I'd like to speak to Stan Foster," I said. I thought if I used his last name, too, it wouldn't send her off into a fit of jealousy.

"May I ask what this is concerning?" She already

sounded suspicious. Good thing I hadn't asked simply for Stan.

"It's a police matter," I said.

That was all right, apparently. "Well, he isn't here yet, but he should be home for dinner any time." Did that mean they were living together? Or maybe she was the type of girlfriend who fixed him candlelit dinners like the one Travis and Nat and I had just had. Well, I hoped not quite like that one.

Suddenly I realized I didn't care if he had romantic candlelit dinners with someone else or not. I'd wondered about that ever since he'd told me he had a new girlfriend. Now I decided I'd really let go. God, I hoped Nat wasn't right—that it was because of Travis.

"May I take a message and have him call you back?" She was proper, too, with all the "mays" instead of "cans." She was a teacher, after all.

I almost blurted out my name, but that would probably have set off alarms that weren't necessary. I deactivated Stan's personal security system by saying "No, I'll call back. I don't know how long I'll be at this number. When do you expect him?"

"He should be here in about twenty minutes. He called and said he was on his way home."

Good. I could catch him on his cell phone.

I hung up and tried that number, but I had to check my Rolodex for it. I had never used it that much.

I could hear traffic noises when he answered on the second ring.

"Are you driving?" I asked.

"Who is this?"

"It's Mandy, and you should pull over to the curb if you're driving." After all, people shouldn't talk on their cell phones when they should be paying attention to the traffic.

"Look, I'm already late for dinner," Stan said.

I knew that, but I didn't say so. "Have you stopped yet?"

I heard what I thought sounded like wheels squeaking to a halt. I resisted the temptation to say that he needed to have his brakes checked, but at least it sounded as if he'd stopped.

"Okay, what do you want, Mandy?"

"Remember the woman I called you about—the one I thought had been murdered although the coroner ruled it an accidental death?"

"How could I forget?"

"Well, I've come into possession of some new information that should make you change your mind about the case."

"What case? And how did you happen to find out information the police couldn't find? Were you snooping again?" I could tell from the way he said it that he was glad we weren't dating anymore.

I tried to act indignant. "If you must know, I hired a private investigator when the police wouldn't follow up." So there, wise guy. "There isn't anything wrong with a private citizen doing that, is there?"

"Well, no." He sounded surprised.

"Anyway, her next-door neighbor, the one who said she knew for a fact that Thelma went down in her basement all the time, is living with a guy named Frank Pankovich. He also has a lot of aliases"—I was reading from the report Travis had given me—"and he has a record a mile long for everything from burglary to blackmail. I talked to his girlfriend—"

"Hold on a minute," Stan said. "I thought you just got through saying you got your information from a private investigator."

One slip of the tongue, and this was suddenly about me. "Okay," I said. "I did have a chat with her because I wanted to satisfy myself that she was right about Thelma and I was wrong. It didn't turn out that way. She told me Thelma went down into the basement all the time. She said she knew because she helped her carry her laundry down there a few weeks before she died."

"What's wrong with that?"

"Because I know it isn't true." I couldn't keep from sounding triumphant. "Thelma had us pick up her laundry because she couldn't get down the steps anymore. We did it for her here at the cleaners."

Stan didn't say anything, and I could hear the hum of traffic in the background.

"Anyway," I said, "her neighbor's boyfriend seemed really suspicious when I was there, so I had this investigator look into him for me before I called you with any more information. He's served time in prison for just the type of thing that happened to Thelma. He could have gone into her house looking for money, and when she discovered him there, he pushed her down the steps and killed her."

"You forgot something," Stan said. "There was no break-in."

That was my trump card. "Yes, but his girlfriend had a key to Thelma's house in case Thelma ever had an accident and needed help. Isn't that ironic?"

"How did you learn that?"

I cringed, but continued, "From another neighbor who used to have the key."

"Christ, Mandy, you haven't changed at all, have you?"

"Well, no," I said. "I believe in finding out the truth when there's been a miscarriage of justice." I sounded so noble I couldn't believe what I was hearing myself say, but I continued. "I think a dear, sweet lady was killed, and you need to look into it."

I took comfort from the fact that Stan finally said, "Okay, give me the name again—the real one and all the aliases."

I spelled them out for him as he wrote them down, probably in the notebook he always kept in his pocket.

"Anything else?" he asked when we were through.

"Well, yes, as a matter of fact there is. Thelma's nephew, Dexter Wolfe, should be checked out, too. He's staying at her house right now. Anyway, his business could be in trouble in Los Angeles because he's in debt to a lot of loan sharks in Vegas. I would say that bears looking into, wouldn't you?"

"And how, pray tell, did you find that out?"

"I didn't talk to him, if that's what you're thinking. The private investigator uncovered that bit of information for me." I realized I'd never told him about the buttons. "I met his girlfriend, though. She came to the cleaners Monday and brought a bunch of old dresses that Thelma wanted me to have. Thelma made the request in a note attached to her will, no less. Well, the dresses were all worn-out, but they had a lot of mismatched buttons on them."

"Back up. What about buttons?"

I had to take a moment to catch my breath. "Thelma

had a button collection sewn on the dresses. Apparently, the buttons aren't worth more than a thousand dollars, but maybe her nephew thought they were. His girlfriend said he didn't even know his aunt. She also said he was disappointed when he got to Denver and found out she didn't have any money. That sounds pretty suspicious to me, like maybe he could have made an earlier trip and killed her for what he thought was his inheritance.''

"Is that all?" Stan asked, and I could tell he hoped it was.

But now that Stan knew I'd been snooping, I didn't have anything to lose with a final admission. "Well, no, there is one other thing. After I'd been over to talk to the neighbors night before last, I'm sure Frank Pankovich followed me to see what I was up to.''

"And how would you know that?" He didn't even sound irritated by this information; I decided I was finally wearing him down.

"Because he was driving a car with only one headlight. Every place I turned, it turned, but I finally got stopped for speeding, and whoever was following me backed off. You can check with the officer because I told him I was trying to get away from a one-eyed car.''

"I don't have to check. I believe you, Mandy." I could almost see him shaking his head at my mischief making. "It sounds just like something you would do. But how do you know it was this Frank Pankovich?''

I made a quick decision to leave out the part about Mack. No sense implicating him. "Well, I went back and checked later, and I saw Frank and his girlfriend turn into her driveway in a car with a burned-out head-light.''

Stan sighed deeply, overriding the traffic whizzing by outside his car. "I don't approve of your methods, but I'll take this up with the department. Okay?"

"Thanks, Stan. That's all I ever wanted." I thought of one final thing. "Oh, and before you go, I wanted to let you know that I called you at home first. I think I talked to your girlfriend, but I didn't tell her who I was. Anyway, she sounded nice. Good luck. You can hang up now."

"You mean I have your permission?"

I smiled. "Sure." He really was a nice guy, but we'd never quite matched. Kind of like a piece of silk and scratchy wool. Want to guess which one Stan would have said I was?

I was feeling good about the conversation with Stan. The matter was now in the hands of the police, where it should have been all the time. I could turn my attention to my own affairs, which I steadfastly refused to think had anything to do with Travis Kincaid or the pesky Nat.

However, I was still pumped up about the information Travis had given me, nothing more, so I turned on the computer and set to work. No sense losing out on an unexpected rush of adrenaline.

I had no sooner booted up the computer than the telephone rang. I tried to decide whether I wanted to answer it or keep working. The call would probably be from Nat, still raving and ranting about Travis. If it was, I would simply hang up on him until he calmed down. I picked up on the third ring.

"Miss Dyer?" a voice said when I answered.

Well, at least it wasn't Nat. He would never address me that formally.

"Yes, who is this?"

"I'm really glad I found you, Miss Dyer. It's Arthur Goldman, and I didn't know where else to turn."

If this was Arthur Goldman, the doll doctor, then the phone call had to have something to do with Betty, and I didn't want to hear it right now.

Arthur was Betty's boyfriend—through no fault of mine, I might add. I'd tried to fix him up with a much more suitable companion at one point, but contrary to all my carefully laid plans, he'd become enamored with Betty. Who can figure the chemistry of love?

"She took my car and went to Boulder," Arthur said.

"Boulder?" Damn. The middle-aged meddler must have gone there to talk to her ventriloquist pal, the guy named Buttons, after I'd explicitly told her that I had no interest in talking to another one of her button experts.

In fact, now that Stan had said he'd look into the matter, I wanted to forget about buttons and bad guys for a while.

"Anyway," Arthur said, "she called a little while ago and wanted me to go up there to get her."

It only took me a second to perceive the problem. "That's ridiculous, Arthur. She has your car."

"But she says she can't see to drive home in the dark."

I knew what my response would have been to that: Then you can wait until daylight, Betty. After all, she'd slept on the street before. This time at least she could huddle up in a car.

I resisted as long as possible any other solution to the problem.

Arthur's voice suddenly dropped to a whisper. ''I'm worried sick about her. To tell you the truth, she sounded as if she'd been drinking.''

FIFTEEN

ARTHUR HAD SAID the magic words—"Betty" and "booze."

I'd taken a small amount of pride—sometimes I wondered why—at getting Betty off the street and off the bottle. I'd given her a job, and against all odds she'd made a life for herself with Arthur. However, I was sure the recidivism rate for bag ladies was high. It would only take a few sips from a shared bottle of wine with her pal Buttons to get her on the skids again.

I thought about this as I drove down Broadway to pick up Arthur for our trip to Boulder. I'd tried to talk him out of going. It was out of my way to go to their apartment to pick him up. But Arthur, one step ahead of me all the time, had said he needed to accompany me. How would he get his car back to Denver otherwise?

Fortunately, it was a relatively warm October night, not one when the Front Range gets an early snowfall. I was glad of that. At least I didn't have to worry about Betty getting hypothermia from a combination of cold and inebriation.

Arthur was waiting for me on the sidewalk in front of the apartment building where he lived with Betty. How could a gentleman—emphasis on "gentle"—who looked like a chubby Kewpie doll find happiness with a rough-cut former bag lady like Betty? This was something I was probably never going to figure out.

"Thank you for coming, Miss Dyer," Arthur said as he climbed into my car and tried to smooth down a wisp of ruffled white hair on top of his head. "I didn't know where else to turn."

Sure, I inadvertently introduce a totally incompatible couple to each other, and all of a sudden I'm responsible for them forever.

I pulled away from the curb. "I didn't realize Betty knew how to drive, much less had a driver's license."

"To be frank with you, Miss Dyer, neither did I."

Oh, great.

Arthur continued, "I usually leave my car at home and take the bus to my shop. I see it as doing my part for the environment as well as a way to cut down on expenses. When I got home tonight, I found a note from Betty saying she had to borrow the car to go to Boulder. Something about helping you out since you wouldn't help yourself."

Oh, yeah, Betty, try to lay the blame on me.

"She's so impulsive when she gets it into her head to do something." Arthur shook his head, but in such an understanding way that I knew it only endeared her to him.

I would have described her actions in far less complimentary terms, perhaps as going berserk when the person she intends to help doesn't want any assistance. Thank you very much.

"Betty takes the bus to work herself, but apparently she hurried home tonight to use the car," Arthur said. "She said it was very important, and she hoped I didn't mind. Of course, that was all right with me because what's mine is hers."

I thought that was a really magnanimous attitude, considering the fact that he wasn't even sure if Betty knew how to drive.

"Do you know what she was planning to do for you?" he asked. "Sometimes she can be a little secretive about such things."

"I have an idea," I said, recalling how she'd stomped out of the cleaners that afternoon. "She wanted me to talk to a guy named Buttons who's a street entertainer on the Pearl Street Mall. Maybe she was planning to bring him back to Denver with her."

Arthur was silent for a while. "I've never heard of anyone named Buttons except for that old-time comedian Red Buttons," he said finally.

"This one's a juggler and a ventriloquist," I said as if that were an explanation.

I pulled onto Interstate 25, which bypasses downtown Denver and the new football stadium, now called Invesco Field at Mile High, where the Denver Broncos play.

"But you said she phoned you after you received the note," I said. "Did I hear you right?"

"Yes, she knew I'd be worried about her, especially once it got dark. She called about seven, and I'd been trying to reach you ever since. I knew you'd know what to do."

What I chose to do at that particular moment was swear silently under my breath.

The traffic was atrocious as I turned onto U.S. Highway 36, a divided highway that veers off Interstate 25 to connect Denver to Boulder.

Arthur kept up a running monologue of worry about Betty as I concentrated on watching the road, ready at any moment to hit the brakes if traffic came to a stop.

"Betty told me about her problem with alcohol when we first met," Arthur said. "I was so proud of her for overcoming it. I just hope this so-called friend of hers doesn't cause her to start drinking again."

I glanced away from the bumper-to-bumper traffic. "I thought you said she'd already been drinking when she called."

"Well, she denied it, of course, but her words sounded a little slurred when she did."

I turned my attention back to the endless rows of taillights, like two strings of red beads in front of me for as far as I could see. Wouldn't it be great if we drove all the way to Boulder and Betty was stone-cold sober?

We came to a standstill where the highway department was doing road work. We had to wait for ten minutes while two lanes of traffic merged into one to get through a work project at an underpass.

It had been several years since I'd been to Boulder, home of the University of Colorado, the heartland of liberalism in the state, and the center of all things New Age. Its residents were also sports-minded and health-conscious and had banned smoking from all public buildings years ago.

Apparently it had been a long time since Arthur had been here, too. "Oh, my," he kept saying of the once-pastoral route between Denver and Boulder, now filled in with housing developments and business parks.

"Good gracious," he said when we passed a giant

new shopping center, called Flatirons Crossing, eight miles out of Boulder.

The shopping center was named for the Flatirons, an outcropping of red sandstone rocks at the southwest edge of Boulder. The rocks had pitched on their sides in some ancient geological upheaval of the mountains and resembled the bottoms of irons, hence the name.

We crested the last rise before Boulder where there was a panoramic view of the city and the foothills beyond. At least there would have been in the daylight. At this time of night, we couldn't see the rock formations, but the lights twinkled from the city as if we were looking down on them from a low-flying aircraft.

"Betty said she'd be down on the Pearl Street Mall," Arthur said. "Do you know where that is?"

Yes, I just didn't know exactly how to get there. I decided to go by the university, where most of the buildings were designed using the same sandstone rocks as the Flatirons.

The area was teeming with students, and we had to wait at a light while they streamed across from the campus to a retail area on what's known as "The Hill."

I'd heard that it was almost impossible to find a parking space in downtown Boulder anymore. The rumor was true. I zigged and zagged around in an awkward rectangle, all because a car couldn't get down or across Pearl Street for a four-block area. It had been turned into a walking mall, popular with students as well as other residents.

As we continued to drive around looking for a parking spot, Arthur became more and more agitated about rescuing his ladylove.

"There's a space," he said, waving his arms toward a gap between two cars where only a bicycle could fit comfortably. After several attempts to back into the space, I gave up.

Betty might be an excellent driver, unknown to either Arthur or me, but I have never mastered the art of parallel parking in a space that is two feet too short for my car. "I'm sorry, but I'm never going to make it," I said as I pulled out of the space for the last time.

Fifteen minutes later, I finally found someone pulling out of a spot in a bank parking lot that was open to the public after banking hours. I had the distinct impression that God didn't want me here. Otherwise She'd have found me a parking space a whole lot quicker.

When I was a teenager, I'd come here once for Halloween. Residents of Boulder and points beyond used to have spontaneous costume parties on the mall. People got dressed up in all manner of weird costumes that were as interesting to spectators as participants. One of my favorites had been a group of people dressed as a complete set of Fruit-of-the-Loom fruits.

The Halloween celebration had finally been banned from Boulder because it tended to get out of hand as the night wore on. However, most every day in the fall, there were a few street entertainers in costume on the mall. Today was no exception.

Since Betty had been her usual vague self about where exactly she'd be, we started walking down the mall looking for her. It was as congested with foot traffic as Highway 36 had been with cars.

"Oh, look," Arthur said. "There's a juggler."

Sure enough, a guy on a unicycle was riding around in circles juggling three tennis balls.

"I don't think he's the one we're looking for," I said. "Our guy is supposed to wear a suit with buttons all over it."

We also saw a man on stilts and several musicians as we made our way along the mall. But where was Buttons? Probably off in some alley hitting the bottle with Betty.

"There he is," Arthur said, waving excitedly the way he'd gestured toward the too-short parking space.

All I could see were what looked like bowling pins twisting through the air. A crowd was gathered around them, and I prayed Betty was among the spectators.

I elbowed my way into the crowd. It wasn't too hard since it was only two deep. Arthur followed in my wake.

"That must be the juggler," Arthur said, getting a glimpse of him. "He has buttons all over his clothes."

Sure enough, it had to be Buttons. Not only was he wearing a white-button-covered suit, I could see a dummy wearing a similar bow-bedecked outfit. The dummy was sitting on a suitcase on the ground beside the juggler.

"But where's Betty?" Arthur looked around the crowd for the object of his affection.

I surveyed the spectators, too. She wasn't there. She'd probably already passed out in that alley I'd been thinking about earlier.

Buttons caught all four of the bowling pins in one hand and put them on the ground. He picked up the dummy, who began to speak, but not without a slight movement from Buttons' mouth. "Thanks, folks. We have to take a break now, but we'll be back in half an hour."

He headed over to Arthur and me, his suitcase and dummy in hand. This had to be some form of ESP, or else Betty had described us to him before she passed out.

"Are these your friends?" Bows, the dummy, asked. The doll was staring right at us with a wooden expression on its face, but the ventriloquist was looking over my left shoulder.

I glanced around, and there was Betty. She'd apparently popped out of a doorway nearby where she'd hidden away from us until she had Buttons' attention.

"Knew you'd bring Arthur up here if I made him think I'd been taking a nip of the old grape," she said, grinning at me.

She didn't look the least bit drunk, and if Arthur wasn't mad at being duped, I sure was. She'd obviously known the right button to push, so to speak, to get us to come up here tonight.

I shook my head at the thought that I was turning into a clone of Nat with his cliché-riddled way of speaking. Not to mention that I'd had just about all I could take of buttons in any shape, size, or form.

The Buttons who was now standing before us was tall and thin with blond hair that stood up in gel-treated spikes all over his head. The dummy had yellow yarn for hair, and it went every which way instead of standing on end.

"So this was a setup," I said to Betty.

"Figured it was the only way to get you up here to talk to Buttons."

I looked over at Arthur, who was in the process of giving Betty a hug. He seemed so happy to see her that I decided he hadn't been in on the con.

"This here's Buttons and Bows," Betty said, as if I didn't already know.

"Glad to meet you." Bows' wooden mouth opened as if he were acknowledging the introduction. I figured the greeting went for both him and the guy who was throwing his voice since I could see the ventriloquist's lips at work again.

"So now that we're here, what?" I asked.

"You need to talk to them. They might be able to help you about the buttons."

"Let's go over to that restaurant, where we can have something to drink." It was Bows again, and I swear he motioned to a pizza parlor nearby.

I really hated this—being directed where to go by a dummy.

"So what can you tell me, Buttons?" I said, refusing to look at the dummy once we sat down in a corner booth of the restaurant. We were lucky to get it because the place was crowded.

"Oh, Buttons says it's better if you talk to Bows," Betty said.

"What?" I yelled loud enough to turn a few heads at a table in the middle of the room.

"Yeah, he likes to talk through his dummy. He says it makes him think better," Betty said.

"Besides, it gives him practice," the dummy said.

This time I could hardly see Buttons' lips move, but I'd had enough. "I think I'll just leave you people here," I said, starting to get up from the booth. "Arthur can drive you home, Betty, when you're through playing around.''

"No." Bows swiveled his head, which I guess was the equivalent of shaking it. "Betty wants me to tell you about the buttons with the secret compar'ments in them.''

I sat back down, but I have to confess, I felt about as stupid as if I were an interloper on Sesame Street and had been persuaded to have a conversation with Kermit the Frog. I, of course, would play the part of Oscar the Grouch.

SIXTEEN

"OKAY, BOWS, SHOOT," I said, glaring at the dummy. Bows gave me a glassy-eyed stare in return.

"Tell her about Buttons' suit first," Betty said, really getting into this make-Mandy-look-foolish thing.

"I'd rather just cut to the part about the hidden compartments in buttons," I said.

The beribboned dummy turned his head away from me. I gathered this was meant to convey that Bows was sulking and wouldn't talk unless he could accommodate Betty's request first.

"Isn't he cute?" Arthur said.

Well, of course, Arthur would feel that way about the dummy. He was a doll doctor, after all, and was into restoring all manner of dolls—everything from Barbies and Cabbage Patch dolls to marionettes and puppets, and perhaps even an occasional dummy like Bows.

"Please." I looked over at the ventriloquist for help in getting to the information about secret hiding places in buttons.

He shrugged. It made some of the buttons on his jacket click together. They were all mother-of-pearl or the equivalent in various sizes, just like the ones we had in profusion back in our alteration department. They were sewn on his jacket so that they made a swirling pattern, kind of like a whirlpool that was try-ing to pull me under. They also looked as if they made Buttons' jacket as heavy as a suit of armor.

I turned back to the dummy and snarled, "Okay, tell me about Buttons' suit."

Just then, a waitress came over to the table to take our orders. She must have thought I was nuts, being nasty to a doll.

Buttons, Betty, and Arthur ordered Cokes and agreed to split a pizza with everything on it. I asked for coffee.

"Nothing for Bows tonight," Buttons said, pointing to the dummy.

They must be frequent customers. The woman didn't even blink an eye.

"You're really very pretty," the dummy mouthed as soon as the waitress was gone.

"Moi?" I was shocked to realize I was actually responding to the dummy's flattery. I had suddenly turned into Miss Piggy from Oscar the Grouch. If I didn't watch myself, I might start batting my eye-lashes. I tried to get a grip. "Now about the suit."

"It's just like the ones that are worn by the Pearly Kings and Queens of England," Betty said.

"The what?"

"They're London's cockney royalty," Betty contin-ued as if she were one of the heirs to the throne.

If she was going to tell me about them, why did I have to come all the way to Boulder? I looked at the ventriloquist. "So are they buskers, too?"

He didn't respond.

"No, they started out belon'in' to guil's," the dummy said.

"Gills?" I asked because the dummy's enunciation left a lot to be desired. I guess that was his human partner's fault, because he had to mumble to keep from moving his lips.

"Guilds," Bows said, but this time I saw Buttons' lips move in order to pronounce the *d*. "Like tray un'ons."

"A tray of onions?" I asked.

"No, trade unions," Buttons said, and he gave up entirely on having the dummy speak. "Originally they sold fruits and vegetables, but nowadays the groups are more like service organizations that do charitable work for good causes."

"Okay," I said, hoping this was the end of the discussion about the Pearly Kings and Queens of England.

"And the kings and queens have the name of their particular organization written on the back of their clothes." At this, the ventriloquist got up and showed me how the name Buttons was spelled out in buttons on the back of his jacket. "And they always have hats, too."

He reached inside his suitcase and pulled out two sailor-type hats, plopping the smaller one on top of the dummy's head. It was covered with ribbons, the same way that his hat was covered with buttons.

"We only wear them when we're doing our ventriloquist act," he said.

The waitress returned with the drinks and set them on the table.

I waited until she left. "About the hidden compartments," I said. I'd been patient for a whole lot longer than Miss Piggy would have been. She'd have bopped Buttons and Bows out of the booth long ago.

Apparently, the ventriloquist realized I was getting to the end of my patience. "Show her your button, Bows."

This was getting more and more weird.

Buttons raised the dummy's hand so that it pointed in the general direction of a button. It was almost hidden away in the center of a big white bow at the neck of his white suit.

"Well, isn't he cute?" Arthur said again.

"I knew you'd like the dummy, Artie," Betty said. "Now aren't you glad you came?"

Arthur nodded happily, but I was reserving judgment.

I leaned down close to the dummy so I could get a better look at the button. It was a military issue that looked as if it was off an army uniform. There'd been a similar button on one of Thelma's dresses.

Could it be that I was really going to find out something useful in this most surrealistic of all worlds?

"It's got a secret compar'ment," the dummy said, practically biting off my nose when his mouth began to go up and down.

I drew back from him quickly. "You're kidding."

"No, they're called locket buttons, and at one time Japanese artists made carved ivory buttons that the owners could use to carry around their opium," Buttons said, apparently having decided that this information was too complicated to convey through his dummy. "As for military buttons, soldiers in the Civil War carried gold pieces in them as ransom if they were captured."

"But this doesn't look like it's from the Civil War."

"No, it's from World War I. Soldiers could use them to hold pictures or even poison capsules in case they were captured.

"In World War II, buttons were even made with tiny compasses in them and were issued to some American and British flyers and paratroopers so they could get their bearings if they got lost behind enemy lines."

"Can you open yours?" I asked.

The ventriloquist took his fingers and quickly popped it open. "I bought my button for three hundred dollars, and I have my name and address inside in case Bows ever gets lost."

I wondered how anyone would even know there was a secret compartment inside. I certainly would never have thought of it. I was glad I didn't say anything about it to the ventriloquist, however. He seemed secure in the belief that, like a tag on a dog's collar, the note inside the button would insure that Bows would be returned to him in the event the dummy ever decided to strike out on its own.

"Ain't that a kick?" Betty asked. "I heard you talkin' with that lady about the uniform button on those dresses you had. I bet it has a hiding place just like this one."

The only way Betty could have overheard my conversation with Mitzi was if she'd been snooping outside my office door after I'd expressly ordered her to go back to work in the laundry. I would have to reprimand her about that later.

"That's sure where I'd hide a message if I didn't want everyone to see it," Betty said.

I drank some coffee, and my adrenaline, which had been at an all-time low, began to pick up. Remote as the possibility seemed, I couldn't help wondering if Thelma could have hidden a note inside a secret compartment in her military button.

"Hey, thank you, Buttons." Frankly, I'd never expected to utter those words in the same breath as his name.

He put his hat out in the gesture of a panhandler or, I guess, a busker. I slipped a twenty in it; the money seemed to satisfy him.

I looked over at Betty. "I just have one question," I said. "Why couldn't you have told me about this without dragging us up here to Boulder? It would have saved Arthur and me a lot of trouble."

For once, Betty looked embarrassed. "I had to have some way to get Artie's car back home. I can't see nothin' at night. I'm blind as a bat."

"That's all right, sweetie," Arthur said. "We're just glad you're okay, and it's been a lot of fun."

Speak for yourself, Arthur. I still wasn't ready to praise Betty for her sobriety or to forgive her for making us come to Boulder. Not unless a secret compartment in the button back in my office actually did turn out to bear a message from Thelma. Maybe not even then.

The waitress returned at that moment with the large pizza the rest of the group had ordered. They dug in with enthusiasm, all except for the dummy and me. I jumped up from the booth. "I'm leaving now. I trust I'll see you at work tomorrow, Betty."

She dropped her slice of pizza. "I wanna come with you." She tried to climb out from the back of the booth even though her boyfriend blocked her way.

I shook my head. "No, Arthur came all the way up here with me to get you. The least you can do is show him where his car is and accompany him back home."

"Yes, we've caused Mandy enough trouble for one night," Arthur said, always the gentleman. "Thank you, Mandy."

Betty frowned at him as if she wished she hadn't made him the middleman in her distress call. "But it was worth it, eh, boss lady?"

"I'll decide about that later."

"Well, maybe we can stop by at the cleaners on our way home to see what you find out." She gave Arthur a pleading look. "We can do that, can't we, Artie?"

Before he had a chance to respond, I said, "It's been a long night for all of us. I, for one, am going home so I can try to get a little sleep. We can check the button tomorrow."

Betty looked so disappointed it did my heart good. I was glad to know I was upsetting her plans for what was left of the evening.

"Thanks again, Buttons," I said:

"Oh, no, thank Bows," the ventriloquist said, motioning to his dummy. "It was really his idea to tell you."

I couldn't believe I was really doing this. "Thank you, Bows." I hurried out of the restaurant before I got stuck with the bill for the drinks and pizza.

On the way back to Denver, I took a fiendish delight in the fact that I had lied to Betty. In fact, I felt so good about it that I didn't even itch.

There was no way I was going to go straight home despite my proclamation to Betty. I knew I would never be able to sleep until I took a look at Thelma's military button.

I headed for the cleaners like a homing pigeon. As soon as I got there, I hurried inside and started tearing through Thelma's dresses, still in a pile at one end of the sofa.

Once I found the right dress, I quickly zeroed in on the uniform button. It didn't look as if it had a hidden compartment inside, but neither had the one the ventriloquist had shown me.

I had a lot more trouble trying to open it than Buttons had when he'd pried open the one on the dummy's suit. I used a letter opener, a fingernail file, and finally just my finger. My nail broke down to the quick, so I walked around sucking on my bleeding finger and cussing my clumsiness. Aha, the file. I finally used it to smooth down the rough edges of my nail as best I could.

If I'd been a soldier trying to open his button's secret compartment to get at his poison, I would have been captured by now and in the process of being tortured for the secrets I knew. Not to mention what would have happened if I'd been lost behind enemy lines and fumbling to get out my miniature compass. I'd have been wandering around in circles and muttering to myself by now. As a matter of fact, that's just what I *was* doing.

I sat back down and stared at the uniform button. I'd told myself all the way back from Boulder that the chances were remote that Thelma even had one of the so-called locket buttons, much less had placed something inside it for my eyes only.

I cussed myself out for not going home instead of coming to the plant. All because I wanted to inspect the button without Betty peeking over my shoulder. If I hadn't been so intent on checking out the button when she wasn't around, I could have been in bed by now, even if I wasn't asleep.

Who was I kidding? Nothing could have kept me from coming here tonight, and since I was here, I decided to give the button one last try, and if my best effort didn't work, I would give up and acknowledge that sometimes a button is just something to hold a soldier's jacket together.

This time the back popped open as if I'd found the magic combination to a locked safe. Go figure. And wonder of wonders, there was actually something inside. Was this my lucky day or what? I was sure Thelma had left me a clue that would identify her killer or at the very least explain where she had hidden a treasure that someone coveted enough to kill for.

The clue, as I'd quickly come to think of it, was actually a tiny scrap of paper folded several times to fit inside the small enclosure. With trembling hands and my torn fingernail, I pulled the slip of paper out of its hiding place and unfolded it.

I could see words printed on the thin strip of paper, apparently with a soft lead pencil. The letters had smeared where the note had been folded in on itself. The paper was torn a little at the front edge as if there might originally have been something that preceded what was there.

I had to squint and turn the paper to the light to make out the message. It read: "not in a buttonhole." Underneath in even smaller letters was "key/rock."

Damn. What kind of clues were those?

SEVENTEEN

I ANSWERED MY own question. The words formed no clues at all. At least not as far as I could see. More than half of Thelma's buttons were sewn on fabric where there were no buttonholes. Big deal.

And what did "key/rock" mean? If it meant the key to the crime was in a rock—maybe an agate that was the centerpiece of one of the buttons—I didn't see how it could be worth enough to justify all my effort, much less lead to murder.

My immediate reaction was to crumple up the slip of paper and throw it across the room. Only trouble was it didn't have enough weight to go very far or be an effective method of demonstrating the temper tantrum I was about to have.

Finally I folded it up just the way it had been and put it back in its hiding place. Then I snapped the button shut, grabbed the dress it was sewn to, and decided the wisest course of action would be to go on home. Not that I would be able to sleep. I was on too much of an adrenaline high, but it was one that was triggered by frustration, not the satisfaction of having discovered something that would help solve the crime.

What the hell did the note mean, anyway? I wasn't familiar enough with Thelma's handwriting, especially her printing, to tell if she was the person who had written it. The letters were a little shaky. That might indicate that the note had been written by an eighty-six-year-old woman like Thelma. But what about a very nervous GI? Nope, it couldn't have been composed by a soldier in battle or even back in the barracks. Not with the reference to buttonholes—unless the note was a reminder that his cyanide pill had been sewn elsewhere into a seam of his uniform.

I thought about the message and even tried saying the words aloud: "Not in a buttonhole." Okay, some of the buttons in Thelma's collection were sewn to the dresses where there were no buttonholes. So far, so good. Did that mean there was a valuable button someplace where there wasn't a buttonhole? One that my resident experts, Les the Rag Man and Mitzi the button collector, had missed or lied about?

And come to think of it, why hadn't Mitzi mentioned the possibility of a secret compartment in the button when she'd talked about the uniform buttons and their relatively modest value? Maybe she didn't know that much about them. Her area of expertise appeared to be presidential buttons, just as Genevieve of the country club set seemed to have a hankering for Bakelite buttons and one especially hard-to-find George Washington inaugural button.

Could Thelma's army button with its secret compartment be coveted by some button collectors just the way it was? Buttons the Busker had said he'd paid three hundred dollars for his dummy's button. That certainly wasn't enough to kill someone for.

I stared at the dresses and the buttons in between the buttonholes. It wasn't getting me anywhere, and it was giving me a headache. When I finally tore myself away from my almost hypnotic trance of button watching, I actually did go home. However, I left Thelma's locket button and the dress it was attached to at work so I could show it to Mack the next morning.

"YOU DON'T LOOK so good," he said when I came in the back door of the plant at the crack of dawn.

"I didn't sleep too well," I said.

Mack went on alert. "Why not? What have you been up to now?"

I looked around for Betty. Apparently, she wasn't here yet. "Come into my office. I want to show you something."

Mack pushed several controls on the cleaning machine to start a load of clothes so it would be ready soon after the pressers came to work. Then he followed me to my office.

I showed him the locket button, and after some difficulty getting it open, the message inside.

"Well, I'll be damned," Mack said. "How did you find out about this?"

I launched into an abbreviated account of Betty's manipulations to get me to Boulder. I even told him the demeaning part about how I'd been forced to talk to a ventriloquist's alter ego, his dummy, in order to extract any information at all.

Mack found it so amusing that I was glad I hadn't shared the even more embarrassing part of my evening activities with him. God forbid that I'd have told him about my dinner with Travis and Nat—the bully and his rabble of victims, myself included.

"So what would you guess the note means?" I

asked after he got over his enjoyment at my misadventures.

"Well, if I were to take it literally, I would say it meant there was a valuable button somewhere on the dresses where there wasn't a buttonhole," Mack said. "But didn't you say Thelma liked word games and plays on words? Maybe she meant something else."

"But what?"

Mack shrugged. "I think that's something we're going to have to think on for a while."

I returned the note to its hiding place. "What do you think I was doing last night? That's why I couldn't sleep."

Mack failed to show sympathy for my bout with insomnia. "So what does the note do to our theory that Frank Pankovich might have killed Thelma?"

I'd been so focused on the message in the button that I'd almost forgotten about Frankie. What *did* it do to our theory? I decided I'd have to tell him what Travis found out after all.

"The private investigator called last night," I said. If Mack got the impression it was a telephone call instead of a personal visit, then my careful phrasing had been successful. "He said Frankie had served time back in Illinois for burglary and blackmail. I already called Stan and told him about it."

Mack nodded his head approvingly. "You did the right thing turning the information over to the police. Let them handle it from here on out."

"I suppose I should call Stan again and tell him about the note, but I hope it doesn't make him dismiss Frankie as a suspect."

"Don't see why it should," Mack said. "Didn't you

tell me Thelma had thought there was a prowler outside her house just before you were there? If Frankie thought there was something valuable in the house—maybe he didn't even know what he was looking for—he could have snuck inside to search for it, using his girlfriend's key.''

I nodded. I was reassured by Mack's words, but I really needed to go back to Thelma's neighborhood to talk to her friend Willetta. This time, I would have to admit who I really was instead of saying I was a distant relative of Frankie's girlfriend, Naomi. But would Willetta still be willing to talk to me once I confessed that I'd been there under false pretenses before?

I needed to think about how I was going to approach her, but right now I faced a busy day ahead. Sadly, it was about to go from busy to impossible.

Betty knocked on the door just as Mack got up to leave. ''So what'd you find out, boss lady? Ain't Buttons and Bows a kick in the pants? Knew you'd love 'em when you finally got to meet 'em. Artie sure did.''

No, what I would really have liked to do was give Betty a kick in the pants right out of my office. She didn't even give me time to form a more tactful request.

''Did that button of yours have a secret compartment inside like Buttons' did?'' she asked.

I steeled myself for a bout of itching. ''Sorry, it wouldn't open. Apparently it isn't one of the locket buttons.''

Betty started for the couch where the dresses were piled. ''Well, let me have a look at it. I bet I can get it open.''

Mack must have decided to stick around. He eased back down in his chair.

"No, Betty, stop," I said. "Okay, it did open, but there wasn't anything inside."

Betty was not persuaded. "I want to see it."

"Later, Betty. Right now I have to get to work and so do you."

Mack stood up and took Betty by the arm, ready to leave.

She resisted. "Promise?"

"All right. I promise."

As soon as they departed, I closed the door and removed the slip of paper from the locket button to a desk drawer that I always kept locked. The last thing I needed was for Betty to go blabbing the contents of the note all over the plant.

In between bouts of Betty-induced itching, I managed to dial Stan's number at the police department. I was pleased when I reached him.

"It's me again—Mandy," I said.

I thought I heard him groan. "I haven't done anything about the information yet. I'm waiting for a call from the coroner's office for more details before I take it up with the sergeant."

"That's not why I'm calling. I wanted to tell you that I found a note inside one of the buttons." Perhaps I should have thought out what I was going to say more carefully and prefaced my news with an explanation of locket buttons.

"I've heard of notes in bottles, but you're the only person I know who could find one in a button," Stan said.

I filled him in on what I'd learned about locket buttons, although I left out the part about Boulder and my conversation with a dummy.

"So what was in this button of yours?" he said.

I gave him the exact wording of the note.

"Sounds like one of those riddles we used to ask each other as kids: What's black and white and read all over?"

"A zebra with a sunburn, right?"

"What are you talking about?"

"The puzzle. Oh, you mean r-e-a-d, not r-e-d, don't you? Well, anyone knows that's a newspaper."

"Actually, I wasn't asking you the question, Mandy."

"Sorry, I guess I just got carried away." I paused. "Anyway, I think the note confirms the fact that Thelma had something valuable—"

"It doesn't sound that way to me."

"Okay, but I just thought you should know, and I still think Frank Pankovich is worth investigating as a suspect in her death."

"Good-bye, Mandy. I'll let you know if anything comes of this."

"Bye." I got the distinct impression that he hoped he wouldn't hear from me in the meantime.

I guess it was Stan's reference to the riddle about the newspaper that made me think of Nat. Maybe I should call him before I went up to the front counter to help with the morning rush. No, I was still mad at him, and besides, I was more bothered by the red/read part of the puzzle. Was I missing something like that in Thelma's note?

I didn't have time to think about it, though. Reluctantly I headed up front, but as soon as I popped out of my office, Betty spotted me.

"Can we look at the button now?"

I decided she would never give up until I gave her a private viewing. I motioned her into the room, opened the button, and let her see the secret but now empty compartment.

"Satisfied?" I asked.

To my surprise, she nodded and returned to the laundry without another word. I followed her, detouring to the front of the plant.

I'd no sooner arrived at the counter than Ann Marie glanced over at me. "You're wanted on the phone." She covered the mouthpiece with her hand and whispered, "It's a man." She said it as if she were surprised that a man would be calling me. Never mind that half our customers are male.

Fully expecting it to be one of them with a problem about a stain we didn't get out of one of his suits, I grabbed the phone. "This is Mandy Dyer."

"This is Travis Kincaid. I was wondering if the information I gave you last night was what you needed or if you want me to pursue any further inquiries." He had a deep, sexy voice on the telephone, as if he were saying one thing and suggesting another.

"No, that was fine." I made my own voice as businesslike as possible. "I turned the information over to the police. Do you usually do follow-up calls with your clients?"

"Not usually, but I didn't have a chance to discuss it once Nat showed up at dinner."

"Oh."

"Is he always that nervous?"

I obviously wasn't about to tell Travis that Nat's nervousness stemmed from the fact that he thought I was two-timing Frankie Panky with Nat's nemesis from grade school.

"Yes," I said finally.

I guess that went with the childhood picture Travis still had of Nat. "Okay, I just wondered. If there's anything else I can do for you, let me know."

I hung up, feeling strangely disappointed by the reason for his call. God, what had I hoped for? That he had called to ask me out for another dinner that wouldn't take place under the watchful eye of Nervous Nat?

"Whoever that guy was, he does good phone," Ann Marie, who's still in her boy-crazy phase, said. "Is he as much of a hunk as he sounds?"

I ignored her and turned to the customer she should have been waiting on instead of listening to my conversation.

WHEN THE MORNING rush was finally over, I retreated to my office to work on the computer data that I'd planned to do the previous night. Betty waylaid me when I was almost there. "Hey, I had an idea. Maybe we should check the other buttons to see if they have secret compartments in them."

"No, Betty. We *both* have other things to do."

I'd only been working about ten minutes when Betty popped into the room. "I was on my way to take my break, but I thought of somethin' else. After you left in such an all-fired hurry last night, Buttons said he could come down here to look at the buttons.

Maybe he could find another secret compartment—since we're both so busy. Want me to call him?''

"No, Betty, all I want is some peace and quiet.''

"Whoops," she said, putting her finger to her mouth and making an exaggerated "Shhhhh" sound. "I'll let you think on it and come back later.''

I waited until she was safely in the break room. Then I collected my things and headed for the back door. I stopped only long enough to tell Mack I was going to be at home in case anyone wanted me. "I'll be back at five, and maybe after we close I can get some work done.''

"Good idea. Like I said, you look as if you can use some sleep. I'll take care of things here.''

I flirted with the idea of going to see Thelma's next-door neighbor, but I talked myself out of it. I was too chicken to admit that I'd lied the first time I'd been to her house.

When I got home, Spot, my fickle feline friend, was as irritated to see me as I'd been to see Betty earlier that morning. He didn't take kindly to a disruption of his routine. Normally he had free run of the apartment six days a week, but we'd worked out a truce for days like this. That meant I lured him off my sofa bed with some of the very expensive cat food I saved for special occasions. While he was eating it, I set my alarm for four-fifteen, then opened the bed and went to sleep.

Just talking about the note with Mack and Stan had somehow eased my mind, and I no longer was fixated on solving a puzzle that might not even exist.

In fact, only an occasional button flitted through my dreams, and I awoke to the alarm four hours later ready to go back to work and hit the books. Some of my enthusiasm came from the fact that I knew Betty would be gone by the time I got there. She went home at four o'clock.

I HELPED AT the counter until closing time, and once the few remaining employees were gone for the day, I went to my office, turned on the computer, and set to work. Only an occasional car passing through the parking lot disrupted my concentration. Traffic was always busy at night with customers going to or leaving Tico Taco's or the nearby liquor store in the strip shopping center behind the cleaners.

It was long past midnight when I finally shut off the computer and called it a day. I'd gone from pumped to pooped in the last few hours, but at least I felt a sense of accomplishment at getting caught up on all the paperwork for once. I should do this more often instead of trying to squeeze it in around the countless interruptions that filled my days.

I slipped into my coat, grabbed my shoulder bag, and headed for the back door. All the businesses in the shopping center behind our plant would be closed by now, and I didn't particularly like walking from the cleaners to my car alone at this time of night, despite the light over the back door.

After I checked the plant's alarm system, I grabbed my keys so I'd be ready to unlock the car as soon as I reached it. Holding the keys firmly in my hand, I prepared to make a run for it. I opened the door, but the moment I crossed the threshold, I came to a dead stop.

Parked a few yards in front of me, poised as if to run me down, was a red-and-white convertible just like the one Frank Pankovich drove.

EIGHTEEN

I SLIPPED BACK inside the cleaners, locked the door, reset the alarm, and waited for my breathing to quit coming out in gulps.

Maybe it wasn't Frank Pankovich's car. With its headlights off, there was no way of knowing if it had a telltale burned-out headlight on the right side. It could have been someone else's red-and-white convertible. But how many old red-and-white convertibles could there be?

Without turning on the overhead lights in the plant, I used the dim illumination from the front of the building to stumble back to my office.

The only window in the room was a small opening high on the wall near the ceiling. All I could normally see from it was a patch of sky, which was just as well. Otherwise, I probably would have spent half my time staring out at the parking lot instead of getting my work done. Never mind what I would have done if I'd had a panoramic view of Denver's skyline the way Travis Kincaid did.

I shut the door of the office, pulled my desk over to the window, and used my chair as a stair step to climb onto the desk. I could barely see over the sill by standing on tiptoe, but my perch afforded me a view of the car.

Nothing moved in the parking lot. The car's top was up, so I couldn't see inside. Was Frankie waiting in it for me to leave? Or was he wandering around outside in the dark, trying to get inside the plant to attack me? Even worse, had he climbed up in the Dumpster on the other side of the window and spied on me while I worked? I shuddered at the thought of someone, especially Frankie, staring in at me.

Thank God, I'd put bars over the window and hooked it into our security system several years ago after someone had broken into the plant that way.

But what if Frankie was just giving me a taste of my own medicine—staking out the plant the way I'd staked out Naomi's house to see what he and his girl-friend were up to? Wait a minute. My mind ground to a screeching halt. Frankie didn't know who I was or where I worked. How could he be waiting for me out-side the cleaners?

I could only think of two ways that could have hap-pened. Either the police had already talked to him in the brief time since I'd dumped my information in Stan's lap or else he'd gotten together with his next-door neighbors, Deke Wolfe and Leilani.

The first possibility seemed unlikely. The police surely wouldn't have told Frankie where the infor-mation originated. Besides, Stan had indicated he would let me know if the police decided to reopen the case.

But what about getting the information from Thel-ma's nephew? Perhaps I'd made a mistake by saying that I was looking for Deke when I knocked on Fran-kie and Naomi's door. If they'd described me to Deke's girlfriend, Leilani, maybe she'd made the con-

nection. After all, I'd acted very interested in how
Thelma died when Leilani brought me the bags of
clothes, and Leilani obviously knew my place of business.

I climbed down from the desk and went over to the
sofa, still in the dark. I moved all the dresses aside
and wondered again about Thelma's unusual request
that I be given the dresses. My mind detoured from
that to my current predicament. I was being held hos-
tage in my own cleaners by a mysterious car in the
parking lot.

I could call the police, but what if the car out there
belonged to someone who was at a bar in the neighborhood? What if the car had been abandoned because
it wouldn't start when its owner climbed in to drive it
away? It was certainly old enough to have mechanical
problems.

What if I put in a call to 911 and it turned out to
be a false alarm? Would that discredit me and the information I'd just unloaded on Stan?

I decided to wait until two to see what happened
when the bars shut down. Maybe someone driving an
old red-and-white convertible had been at Tico Taco's
and then decided to have a nightcap in one of the
neighborhood drinking establishments. It must be after
one by now. Not that long a wait.

Fumbling to my office door, I punched in the button
to lock it. I felt relatively safe inside my fortress. The
place had a top-notch alarm system. If anyone tried to
get in it would send a signal to the security company.
The person on duty would call the police.

Meanwhile I could call Nat. Lure him down here
with a promise to tell him the real story of Frankie

Panky. Even tell him the whole thing over the telephone if necessary. I knew he would come at that point, and we could check out the car together. Maybe even have a good laugh when the car was vacant. Just another misadventure to add to our memory book of shared experiences.

The faint light from the parking lot was just enough so I could dial the telephone. Nat's phone rang. If he was there, I knew he'd pick up. Nat never wanted to miss a call about a fast-breaking story that might give him a front-page scoop.

He picked up on the second ring.

"Nat, this is Mandy. I need—"

"I don't want to talk to you." *Bang.*

I called back.

Nat's voice came on the line again. "I have nothing to say to you." *BANG.*

I tried the number a third time.

"This is Nat," his answering machine voice said. "At the beep, leave a message." Except there was no beep. It had been Nat, pretending to be on tape.

After that, the phone rang twenty times. He was apparently so mad that he'd even shut off the machine. That was definitely un-Nat-like. He was really in a snit about this Travis thing. I was tempted to keep calling him all night so he would be forced to put his pillow over his ears and still not be able to get any sleep. It would serve him right.

However, I was too tired to play games with him at this late hour. I climbed back onto the desk and took one more look outside. The car was still there. But nothing moved around or inside it that I could see.

I thought about calling Mack, but I didn't want to

scare him. I worried about him. Not only was he holding down a full-time job here at the cleaners, but he was spending every night directing the upcoming play. He was in his sixties, after all, and I wanted to keep him healthy so he'd keep working at the plant as long as possible. I couldn't get along without him.

What about Travis Kincaid? Oh, yeah, he would really like to come riding to my rescue, wouldn't he, the way he and his girlfriend had when I wrecked Nat's bike? I didn't want to be obligated to him in any way, and besides, he'd probably bring his current lover along with him. Forget that idea.

I went back to the sofa, put my coat over me, and curled up at the end I'd cleared of Thelma's dresses. With my head resting on the arm of the sofa, I finally managed to convince myself that I was letting my imagination run roughshod over my reason. Still, I would wait until after two to see if the car and its barhoppers left. I was sure they'd be gone the next time I looked.

I'd been tired when I turned off the computer. Now I was running on empty. I fell asleep, then awakened with a start. Had I heard something? I was disoriented for a minute about where I was and why I was there.

I heard a police siren in the distance, and the realization hit me that I was hiding in my office. I had no idea how long I'd been sleeping, but the siren's whine was getting closer and closer. Had the security company picked up a silent alarm from here at the cleaners and called the police to check it out? Unfortunately, the patrol car sailed by on First Avenue before I could run out and hail someone. The siren faded away in the distance.

I listened intently for the noise that had awakened me, but the only sounds I could detect were the creaking noises of a building and its equipment at rest.

What time was it? I had a crick in my neck from the way it had been bent while I'd been sleeping. The top of my head felt as if it had gone to sleep, the way an arm or leg does sometimes. Could that really happen?

I massaged my neck, then rubbed the crown of my head as I felt my way to the window. My desk wasn't where it was supposed to be. That's right, I'd never moved it back from the wall. I flipped on the desk lamp with the speed of someone striking a match and snuffing it out again. In the brief moment of light, I squinted at the numbers on my watch. It was the kind of watch that had driven poor Les out of business.

The numbers read 5:37. Good grief, I'd apparently been asleep for four hours. Mack would be here in less than an hour to be ready when the rest of the employees started arriving. This was his week to open up; next week would be mine.

I started to climb back up onto the desk. One more look outside. I was sure the car would be gone. I'd built up the whole Frankie scenario because of the lateness of the hour when I'd started to leave last night. As soon as I checked the parking lot one more time, I would hurry home to feed Spot, shower, and change clothes so I'd be ready to come back to work. Oh, yeah, I really felt like another day of work.

I almost lost my footing. That's what grogginess does to me when I first wake up. I finally managed to get a firm footing on top of the desk, stood on tiptoe, and looked out across the lot.

Damn. The car was still there. I'd had enough. No more hiding inside the cleaners like one of the rabble of victims, frightened of both the bully and the boogeyman. I climbed down from the desk, turned on the overhead light, and grabbed my shoulder bag and coat.

I was going to walk right over and check out the car. Probably it was stolen and someone had dumped it in the parking lot. There must be a market for old convertibles, just as there was for buttons. Without any more fooling around, I would climb into my car and use my cell phone to call the police. I would tell the dispatcher that there was an abandoned car in the lot just off First Avenue.

I adjusted the security alarm in order to get out the back of the plant. Then I hurried through the door and out into the predawn morning. Still, I had a hard time making my feet go over to the convertible. What if it was Frankie in the driver's seat, and he'd fallen asleep the way I had in front of his house? The sensible part of me said, no, that couldn't be. Even I wouldn't have slept in a car all night. But hey, hadn't I just done the same on a sofa with my head propped at a right angle against its arm?

I kept telling my feet to walk up to the car so I could look inside. It would be empty. Then I could run over to my own car, get in it, make my call, and go home. I would never tell Mack or anyone else about spending the night hiding in the cleaners because of an empty car.

I was almost to the convertible. Just as I'd hoped, it was empty. I felt a surge of relief. It had been really dumb of me to let my imagination get the best of me. It had kept me imprisoned in the cleaners all night.

I peeked into the car. Oh, God. There was something in the front seat. Not something. Someone. Maybe the person was drunk, sleeping it off because he'd heeded the warning not to drive and drink.

But what if it were someone who'd had a heart attack and I could have saved him if I'd just gone out and taken a look earlier?

My own heart was in my throat. My breath was coming in raspy gasps because of the blockage to my air passage.

I tapped on the window. No response. I did it again. Still nothing. I went over to the passenger-side door, but I stopped before I grabbed the handle. Be smart. I took a Kleenex out of my purse and used it to hold on to the handle. I yanked on the door.

The person's head, which had been wedged up against the armrest, fell forward toward me. It was Frank Pankovich.

NINETEEN

I DIDN'T KNOW it was Frankie at first. I jumped back from the body as if I were dodging a bullet. When I recovered from the initial shock, I edged back over to the man. Maybe I wasn't too late to help him.

I reached down to check for a pulse, and that's when I saw his face and the belt pulled taut around his neck. I couldn't believe it. This time I stumbled backward, falling to the pavement as I tried to get away.

It couldn't be Frankie Panky. What had he been doing that could possibly have gotten him killed just outside my dry cleaners? I was in a full-blown panic now. I kept scooting backward on the ground, then turned and half crawled away from him. I finally managed to struggle to my feet about the time I reached the door of the plant. It was a good thing I had it as support, or I probably would have collapsed in a heap on the threshold.

Obviously, I had to call the police, but what was I going to tell them? How could I possibly explain that a man I'd just fingered as a suspect in Thelma's murder—a murder that no one but me suspected—was now dead at my doorstep?

Maybe I should call Stan first. I was afraid I'd get the kindergarten teacher. I needed to call him anyway. I had to tell him to forget everything I'd told him the other night. No, I couldn't ask him to lie, mainly because I knew he wouldn't do it. As an alternative, I could tell him the truth—that I was in a world of hurt and he should get himself down to the cleaners right away. I rejected that idea, too.

Why not just get in my car and drive away? I'd been smart enough not to leave my fingerprints on the door handle. Let someone else report the crime. The first person to pull into the parking lot would be sure to see Frankie's head dangling out of the front door. No one could miss it.

Suddenly an even scarier thought occurred to me. The first person on the scene would probably be Mack. He would be in as much trouble as I was. More maybe. He was black, and that's what racial profiling was all about, wasn't it? Besides, he'd been the one who'd come to my rescue when I was staked out at Naomi's house. He and his pickup with the vanity plates "MAC TRK" might have drawn a lot more attention from Naomi and the dog walker than even I had.

I made up my mind. I couldn't risk Mack's being the one to find the body. In fact, I needed to call the police before he got here. And should I tell the cops that I knew the name of the victim? Would they believe me when I said he didn't know my name, much less my place of business? No one would buy that. It was too much of a coincidence for even me to swallow. But it was the truth, wasn't it?

How could Frankie have wound up here in the first place, never mind dead? And with a belt twisted around his neck? A belt. Suppose the police decided I'd gone outside and slipped into the backseat for a prearranged meeting with the skinny little hooligan?

A belt would have been an easy enough thing for me to grab on the way out of the cleaners to use as a weapon.

Get a grip, Mandy. Remember, you're not the guilty person here. You're the one who's trying to see that justice is done for your friend. Just call the police. Let them figure it out.

Like someone in a trance, I dug around in my purse until I found my cell phone. I could just as easily have gone back inside the cleaners to make the call, but that's why I'd finally purchased the cell phone—for an emergency. I leaned against the back door for support and tried to remember how to dial 911 on the cell phone. Depress the ''1'' and wait. That was it.

By the time I reached a police dispatcher, I regretted the fact that I'd stayed outside. If I'd gone to my office, I wouldn't have had to worry about the ghost of Frank Pankovich coming out of the shadows to accost me. Or what if Frankie's killer was waiting to kill me, too?

I tried to shake off the thought, but I couldn't. I saw shapes in the shadows around the Dumpster to the right of the door. I'd broken out in a cold sweat by the time I began to tell the dispatcher that I'd found a body in a parking lot. I gave the address.

"Yes, I'll wait here," I said to the calm female voice on the other end of the line. "Yes, I'll keep holding until someone gets here."

I'll stay on the line, but please, don't try to keep me talking, I prayed. The woman kept talking anyway, but I didn't really hear what she said. I had to try to figure this out. As if I could make sense of it if I had all the time in the world.

I didn't even have five minutes. I heard a siren in the distance, and my thoughts were still as jumbled as when I'd first found the body. The more I thought about it, the less it made sense.

The patrol car slowed as it pulled into the parking lot. I waved and motioned toward the body, then started to walk in that direction. My legs almost gave out on me. It was as if all my blood had pooled down in my feet and I couldn't move.

"The police car is here now. I'm hanging up." I depressed the off button on the phone. "Over here," I yelled at the cop.

The policeman, an officer traveling solo, got out of his patrol car. I flirted with the idea of telling him I'd just arrived at work but decided to tell him the truth instead. This was not the time for the little white lies that might have gotten me into this predicament in the first place. Besides, I'd already spilled everything I knew to Stan.

"I was leaving work, and I saw this car in the parking lot." My words tumbled out the way poor Frankie's head had fallen out of the car. "I thought it might have been stolen and abandoned here, but when I went over to take a look, I saw a man inside. I ran around to this side to see if he needed help, but when I pulled on the door, he—" I pointed at the body, but I couldn't finish.

The policeman identified himself as Officer Hardwick, then bent down and checked Frankie's wrist for a pulse. "He's dead."

I already knew that from the bloated face and vacant eyes.

"Any idea who he is?" the cop asked.

I swallowed hard. "I think his name is Frank Pankovich." I didn't volunteer any other information.

"And what's your name, miss?"

I gave it to him and told him I'd been pulling an all-nighter at the cleaners.

The officer called in the rest of the troops. I didn't know whether to hope that the homicide officer called to the scene would be someone I knew or a total stranger.

Before any of the homicide team got there, a pickup pulled around the side of the building and slammed to a halt beside my car. Thank God, I hadn't followed my first instinct to run. If I had, Mack would have been the one to find the body.

He jumped out of his truck before I could even get to him. "What's going on?" His dark face seemed to pale under the artificial light above our back door.

"I don't know," I said, and fought back tears. "It's Frank Pankovich, and he's dead."

"Christ," Mack said. "What happened?" He wrapped me in a big bear hug as if that would protect me.

"I stayed at work last night, and when I got ready to leave, I saw his ca—." My voice was muffled by the old pea jacket he always wore.

The officer came running over to us. "I don't want you talking to anyone until the detective gets here." He looked at Mack. "And who are you?" Then back at me. "Did you call him to come down here?"

I pulled away from Mack. "He's my plant manager, and he was reporting for work. We open at seven."

"Just go inside then." The officer looked at me. "But you stay here."

Mack followed orders, but I could see all the questions in his eyes. Questions that I couldn't answer even if I'd been allowed to talk to him.

The whole crew of people who respond to homicides began to arrive right after that: paramedics, several other policemen in marked cars, the coroner, the crime scene people.

Officer Hardwick took a brief statement from me that didn't seem to satisfy him. I know because of the way he raised his eyebrows in disbelief as I spoke.

By then two homicide officers had arrived. Unfortunately, I'd met the lead investigator before. His name was Detective Reilly, and he looked like a football player. He'd given me a hard time on the several other occasions we'd met, but at least back then I'd been dating Stan, which had given me a degree of credibility. Innocence by association. Someone to vouch for me. I didn't think that would happen again.

The police were busy roping off an area around Frankie's convertible with crime scene tape. I prayed they wouldn't continue stringing tape around the cleaners. I couldn't afford to have my business shut down while the police investigated the murder.

"You again," Reilly said when he came over to me. I'd been hoping he'd have forgotten me, but no such luck.

He went over my statement in excruciating detail, then said, "I'm afraid we're going to have to take you downtown to try to sort out this information in your statement. It's pretty confusing."

You betcha it was confusing. I didn't know what the hell was going on, and the more I'd told Reilly the more I'd probably implicated myself.

"We're going to need to search your cleaners. Do we have your permission or do we need to get a search warrant?"

Be my guest, I said, although in different words. I supposed they'd be looking for a missing belt from one of our customers' clothes. Lots of luck. It would be like looking for the proverbial needle in the haystack, but I hoped that by being cooperative I would convince the police I had nothing to hide.

"And we'll need to take a look at your car. Is that it?" He looked toward my Hyundai.

I nodded.

"We'll need your keys."

I handed them to him and said I needed to go into the cleaners to tell my plant manager what was going on.

Reilly accompanied me and waited while I told Mack to give the police full access to the building and that I'd be back "whenever." Mack's eyes were filled with a hundred questions, and I still didn't have any answers.

As we left the building, Reilly had a firm grip on my elbow. I wondered if he thought I was going to make a break for it. Or maybe it was because he'd caught sight of Nat.

The ace crime reporter had just zoomed into the parking lot on his motorcycle. Apparently he'd been summoned by the city desk to cover the story, or else he'd heard the report over his police scanner at home. I always imagined that he slept with one eye open, constantly on the alert for any crime that was reported in the city.

He jumped off and made a beeline toward me.

"Keep away from her, Wilcox," Reilly yelled at him.

Nat kept coming, like an airplane on a final approach to a runway.

One of the uniformed officers headed toward him, and for a minute I thought the guy was going to have to restrain Nat.

Reilly whisked me away to a waiting unmarked car, where his partner, a Detective Holmes, did the honors of escorting me to the Denver Police Administration Building downtown. As we left, I noticed that Nat had given up on talking to me. He'd made his way to Reilly and was peppering him with questions.

In the car, I tried to make small talk with Holmes, a tall, thin man with the beginnings of a paunch. At least we didn't have a history the way Reilly and I did.

"Any relation to Sherlock?" I asked.

Apparently he had no sense of humor, or else he'd heard every Sherlock Holmes crack in the book. He glared at me, and we rode the rest of the way in silence.

I'd been to the police building before, and I knew the drill. We went to the Crimes Against Persons offices on the third floor, and Holmes escorted me to an interview room down a hallway.

He was joined in the room by another detective, a woman this time. She introduced herself as Jody Henderson and told me that the interview would be videotaped. I knew that already. Then they began to pummel me with questions, but for the life of me, I couldn't tell which one was playing the bad cop and which the good cop.

I told them the whole story about Thelma's death and my suspicions that she'd been murdered. Then I tried to explain about the old dresses with the mismatched buttons. I explained about the note that I'd "know what to do with them," and how it had raised my suspicions because Thelma had always liked to play word games.

"At first, I thought they might be valuable to collectors, but I finally decided they weren't worth all that much," I said.

"How did you conclude that?" Holmes asked.

I really hated to admit my sources. "Well, a man who used to work in a jewelry store said the buttons didn't appear to have any precious stones in them, and a woman who's a button collector examined the buttons and said they weren't that valuable."

The police finally wrested the names of my authorities from me. It apparently diminished the credibility of the appraisals in their eyes. Before they could move on to something else, I told them about the strange clues inside the locket button.

"What do you think the message inside the button meant?" Henderson asked.

"I wish I knew."

She and Holmes devoted the rest of their interview to my connection to Frankie. They questioned me intensively about my visits to Frankie and Naomi's house and to the house of the other neighbor.

"Why did you lie about the purpose of your visit?"

"I didn't want them to get suspicious about what I was doing there. I just wanted to find out why Naomi told the police that Thelma went down into her basement all the time when Thelma had told me she didn't.

"We did her laundry for her because her washer and dryer were in the basement, yet Naomi said she helped Thelma carry her clothes down there just a few weeks before Thelma's death."

"And you say that you think they were suspicious of you and followed you that night in a car with only one headlight," Holmes said, looking through his notes.

I nodded. "Yes, because I went back the next night to check it out. When they drove up in their driveway, the car had only one headlight." I debated for a minute, and just as I had with Stan, I decided to leave Mack out of it. Probably a big mistake, but Holmes hadn't asked me for corroboration about the story. Besides, I needed someone to keep the cleaners operating if I was thrown into jail on suspicion of killing Frankie.

"I already told Stan Foster all of this."

"You did?" Holmes quit writing. "How do you happen to know him?"

"We dated for a while, and we're still friends." That last part was stretching the truth, but I liked to think Stan would back me up. Besides, it was the best I could do in the way of a testimonial.

Holmes recovered quickly from this bit of information and began to question me about Frank Pankovich. I shared the information I'd learned from Travis about Frankie's record.

"Where did you learn that?"

"Through a private detective I hired."

"What's his name?"

I wondered if the same code of confidentiality applied to both the client and the investigator. I decided it didn't. After all, you give out the name of your doctor or lawyer in similar circumstances. I gave him Travis's name.

"Pankovich had served time in prison for burglary and blackmail," I said, "so I thought he could have been searching Thelma's house and killed her when she discovered him."

"But he's dead now. How do you explain that?"

I couldn't. In fact, that's when the whole interview fell apart.

"I don't know," I repeated over and over as Holmes and his female counterpart continued to shoot questions at me as if they were firing a machine gun.

"Why do you think Pankovich was in the parking lot behind your cleaners?"

"I don't know."

"Do you think he knew it was your business?"

"I don't know."

"How could he have found out your name since you never told him who you were?"

"I don't know."

"Why do you think he was killed behind your business?" Implied in the question was who, besides me, would have had a reason to do it.

"I don't know."

They backtracked and rephrased questions, always with the same answer from me: "I don't know."

Oh, God, I wished I did. And if I were lucky enough to be released, I knew I'd better find out the answers. Otherwise, I might not be free for long.

TWENTY

THE DETECTIVES finally told me I could go. It was nearly noon, and I hadn't been sure up until then that they would actually release me.

"Don't leave town," Henderson said.

"I won't."

My only thought at that moment was to get out of the police building, not out of town.

"I'll take you back to Cherry Creek," Holmes said.

Too bad. I would have liked to walk. Never mind that it was probably five miles. I needed time in the crisp October air to clear my head. Clearing my head in no way equated to being able to figure out what was going on. I knew it would take a lot more than a clear head to do that.

He zipped me back to the cleaners while I tried to rethink everything about Thelma's death. I had no idea where to start. Not now that my prime suspect had turned up dead. Could Deke Wolfe and his girlfriend, Leilani, have had something to do with Frankie's murder? What if Frankie had seen them over at Thelma's just before her death and had been blackmailing them about it?

It was obvious someone had tried to set me up for Frankie's murder. Why else would he have been killed in the parking lot outside my plant? I probably should leave everything to the police, but maybe it wouldn't hurt to go back and talk to Willetta. That's what I'd been thinking of doing the previous day until I chickened out. I still hadn't figured out a way to tell her that I'd lied the other time I'd been there. Not and have her like me, anyway.

I needed to call Stan, too, since I hadn't run into him at police headquarters. I was glad of that. He'd probably be livid if he'd already given my information to his superiors. After all, wouldn't it look strange if he'd given them the information about Frank Pankovich, only to have the man turn up dead in back of my plant?

The cleaners had a Closed sign on the front door when we drove by. Holmes turned into the parking lot, and the police were still there. The forensics team was swarming all over Frankie's car as well as the Dumpster outside my back door. I supposed they were in the plant as well. After all, I'd given them permission.

"Wait here," Holmes said. He went to talk to Detective Reilly.

I looked around for Nat and breathed a sigh of relief when I didn't see him. He could be a real pest when he was being a reporter instead of a friend. Of course, he could be a pain in the butt as a friend, too. Look how he'd refused to take my call last night when I needed him. Well, two could play at that game. See if I'd give him any information now that he probably would want to buddy up to me.

Holmes consulted with Reilly for what seemed like an inordinate amount of time. Then Reilly came over to me. "We're still checking out your place, so we sent all your employees home," he said.

"When can I get back inside?"

"Right now. We want you to show us the dresses with the buttons on them that belonged to Thelma Chadwick. We'll have to take them as evidence."

He escorted me into the cleaners, and I relinquished the dresses. I hated to see them go; I kept wondering if there was a valuable button on them that Les the Rag Man and Mitzi Porter had missed or had misled me about.

"I'll let you know when you can resume work," Reilly said. "Your plant manager insisted on waiting for you at that restaurant behind the cleaners." I knew he was referring to Tico Taco's, where Travis, Nat, and I had spent our disastrous dinner earlier in the week.

Bless Mack. I wanted—no, needed—to talk to him to try to get some perspective on all of this, and I went out the door and headed across the parking lot, skirting the area with the crime scene tape.

I was relieved to see that Manuel was nowhere in sight when I got inside Tico Taco's. As I knew all too well from recent experience, he tended to hover whenever there was any activity going on that he thought he should know about.

Today the restaurant was nearly empty. The police activity in the parking lot had apparently cut down on Tico Taco's normal midday business.

I spotted Mack easily, but I pulled back when I was halfway to his booth. He was talking to someone, and for a moment, I was afraid it was Manuel. Actually, there was a whole host of people besides our host that

I didn't want to see right then. As it turned out, this was one of them. Even Betty would have been preferable.

Travis, of all people, was sitting across from Mack, and they seemed to be hitting it off much better than I would have hoped. All I needed right now was for Nat to show up and make it a foursome.

"How do you know each other?" I asked.

Chalk up my confusion to the events of the last few hours, no food, and a lack of caffeine this morning.

"Travis came in and introduced himself," Mack said. He turned and waved at the waitress who was standing back by the coffee machine. "Bring Mandy a cup of coffee, please."

With some reluctance I scooted in beside him. He looked as if he needed another shot of caffeine himself.

Travis waited until the waitress brought my coffee and topped off the ones he and Mack were drinking. I debated ordering a breakfast burrito, but I decided against it. It would probably just make me throw up.

"I have a friend in the police department," Travis said, "and I had him run a check on Pankovich the day you came to see me. He called me as soon as he heard that the same guy I'd been inquiring about was murdered last night."

I guess it made sense that Travis would want to find out what was going on after I'd asked him to investigate Frankie.

"Someone will probably be calling you again," I said. "I told the police I'd gone to you about Frankie."

Travis shrugged and motioned to the parking lot.

"When the cleaners was closed, the police directed me over here to your plant manager to find out about my clothes." Smart of him to pretend to be a customer. "How'd Pankovich wind up back here behind your place of business?"

"I swear I don't have any idea. I'm sure Mack already told you that. I didn't even think he knew who I was."

Travis gave me a penetrating look, but this time it wasn't the sexy kind. More like he was trying to figure out what I was all about.

I guess I passed his eye-contact test. "As you probably know," he said, "P.I.s can't get involved in ongoing criminal investigations, but if there's anything I can do for you later, call me."

Who did he think he was? The Good Samaritan riding to my rescue on his motorcycle again? I prayed I wouldn't need his help, but he must be assuming that I'd be arrested and my lawyer might need an investigator for the trial. It didn't make me feel any better.

He handed me his card. "This is my home number." He jotted something down on the back. "Call me any time."

I glanced at the card. He had extremely good handwriting for a guy who'd practically flunked out of school.

"Look, I have to get going, and I'm sorry about all this," Travis said. "Nice meeting you, Mack."

I nodded and stuffed his card in my shoulder bag.

"Same to you," Mack said, reaching over to shake his hand. "He didn't seem like such a bully to me," he continued once Travis was gone.

I gave Mack a dirty look, but maybe the comment

afforded him a moment of levity in an otherwise heavy conversation. We discussed the murder in depressing detail, but neither one of us had any theories on why Frankie had been killed outside the cleaners.

"Betty was a real nuisance this morning," Mack said. "She kept wanting to talk about the buttons, so I made certain to get her out of the cleaners as soon as the police said everyone could go. I was afraid they'd suspect her of something, the way she was blathering on about buttons."

"Thanks," I said, "and speaking of the buttons, I had to give the dresses to the police."

Mack nodded. "I've been thinking about that reference to 'key/rock' inside the locket button. I wonder if it could mean that Thelma had a valuable diamond and was trying to tell you about it."

"But 'rock'?" I asked.

"Sure. Don't people say 'Did you see the size of that rock on her hand?' when a man gives his fiancee a huge diamond engagement ring?"

"I suppose." I guess the reason I hadn't thought of it was that the diamond my ex-husband had given me was about the size of a very small pebble. "So where is it? And what does 'not in a buttonhole' have to do with anything?"

Mack shook his head. "I don't know. I guess it means it's somewhere else." We were right back where we'd started. "By the way, I told the police about our stakeout the other night."

"Jeez, Mack, why'd you do that? I was so careful to leave you out when I told them about the one-eyed car."

"I figured that's what you'd do, but someone might

have noticed my license plate and tracked us down that way. I guess I need to get rid of that 'MAC TRK' license plate if I'm going to be sneaking around. Besides, I was the only one who could verify that Frankie was driving a car with a burned-out headlight like the one that was following you.''

Damn. Now the police would probably think Mack helped me kill Frankie when I found him skulking outside the cleaners.

"You know," I said, "we keep thinking that Frankie found out about the cleaners, maybe by describing me to Leilani after I said I was looking for her and Deke. But what if someone who did know about the cleaners set up a meeting with him out in the parking lot? He might not even have realized that the cleaners was connected with the person he'd tried to follow.''

"That's a thought, but who could it be?''

"Deke and Leilani, or one of the countless number of button collectors.'' We were back to square one for a second time.

We continued to discuss Frankie's death until my stomach began to rumble. I finally ordered toast, not Tico Taco's usual fare, to try to soothe it. I think Manuel kept bread on hand just for me. I was often in need of something bland to help me through one of my ulcer-producing days.

Once I'd finished the toast, I finally gave up. "I think we should both go home, Mack. The police said they'll notify me as soon as we can get back into the cleaners.''

"I'll go along with that. It'll give me a chance to rest up for the play. Don't forget, tomorrow is opening night. I got you the best seats in the house.'' He handed me two tickets, but I couldn't think what to do with the second ticket.

I just hoped Mack's premiere performance and our curtain calls didn't coincide.

MACK OFFERED TO give me a lift home, but Reilly said I could have my car back. It had the remnants of fingerprint powder all over it; apparently, the police had been trying to see if Frankie and I had rendezvoused inside the car.

I felt an overwhelming sense of relief when I pulled away from the parking lot, probably the way Travis used to feel when he skipped school, but the feeling didn't last long.

When I opened my apartment door, Spot eyed me as if I were guilty of the most heinous of all crimes—cat abuse. He meowed about my being gone since the previous afternoon and made a big to-do about his kitty dish's being empty, even of the last morsel of dry food. I filled up the dish with both canned and dry food, replenished his water supply, and then took a look at my answering machine. It was full of messages.

I knew I didn't want to listen to them, but I ran the machine back to the beginning anyway.

"This is Stan. What the hell is going on? I came in to work this morning and took up the case of Thelma Chadwick with my boss. I'd no sooner gotten to the part about Frank Pankovich than I found out his body had been discovered behind your cleaners." He paused for a moment, apparently in frustration. "What the hell is going on? Call me as soon as you get in."

I'd never known Stan to be so repetitive with his

swearing, and I wondered why he hadn't shown up in the interview room or the parking lot if he was so eager to talk to me. He probably didn't want to be seen anywhere near me. Guilt by association.

I stopped the machine and called him. He deserved at least that much. I was relieved when I got his voice mail, and I tried to explain everything I'd just gone through telling the rest of the police force—namely, that I didn't know anything.

"Maybe it was just an unfortunate coincidence," I concluded, and hung up. Anyone who believed that would have to have a couple of buttons missing. That's what my Uncle Chet used to say, not realizing what an unfortunate choice of words they would turn out to be.

I turned the answering machine back on. This time the voice was practically screaming, and it took me a moment to recognize the not-so-dulcet tones of Nat.

"Jesus Christ, Mandy, what the hell is going on?" That phrase again. "I couldn't believe it when I heard Frankie was dead. I thought he was your main squeeze until the other night. What did you do—hire Travis to off him?"

I was appalled that Nat would say that.

"Don't worry," he continued. "I haven't said anything to the cops about you and this Frankie guy, and I didn't mean that about you getting Travis to be your hired gun. But what the devil happened? Was it a lovers' triangle or something?"

Now I was beyond appalled.

"Call me," Nat said. "I'll sit on the story until I hear from you."

He didn't have a prayer of hearing from me with an attitude like that.

All the other calls were from Nat as well. By the last message, he'd rescinded his accusation about a lovers' quarrel. He pleaded to know what had happened and even promised that the information would be off the record. This was a concession from Nat that was almost unheard of.

I was still fighting mad, and the last thing I wanted to do was get a bunch more calls from Nat or hang around until he showed up on my doorstep. That's what he always did when he couldn't get me any other way.

Now that Spot had finished eating and no longer seemed ready to bring animal abuse charges against me, I showered, changed clothes, picked up my shoulder bag, and left. I had one more task my brain was telling me to avoid but my gut was telling me I had to do: pay a visit to Willetta Woods no matter what the consequences.

TWENTY-ONE

"Oh, I REMEMBER YOU," Willetta said when she finally answered her door. "You're the angel."

She was referring to the undeserved compliment she'd given me earlier in the week about looking like Roma Downey on the TV show *Touched by an Angel*. The comparison made it doubly hard for me to confess that I'd lied to her that night. After all, angels wouldn't lie.

"Uh—I stopped and bought some Burger Kings," I said, holding up the sack from my fast-food run on the way to her place. "I thought you might like to have one with me."

"Well bless you, child," she said. "Come on in."

I wondered if I should come clean with her before I went inside. That way, she'd have the opportunity to turn me away at the door. On the other hand, I didn't know when a patrol car might cruise by, and I didn't really want to be seen lolling around outside. I'd already scoured the area for signs of the police, but they'd apparently come and gone or hadn't even been here yet.

The heavyset black woman was wearing a muumuu and the same men's slippers she'd had on before. I thought she was walking a little better than she had the other time, but her ankles still looked swollen.

Once I was inside, she motioned me to sit on the sofa again.

"Let me get us some plates from the kitchen," she said.

"No, I'll be glad to do that." Anything to stall my confession as long as I could.

She sat down heavily in her chair. "They're in the cupboard."

I found them easily and returned to the front room.

"Well, this is a pleasant surprise," she said. "We can pretend we're having a picnic."

It was no picnic for me. "Look, Willetta. I have a lot of things I need to tell you."

"I was hoping you might," she said.

Her answer caught me off guard. I sat down across from her and started putting the burgers and French fries on our plates. I set the soft drinks I'd brought on a couple of napkins. "What do you mean?"

"Naomi said she didn't have a relative named Bonnie Fitzgerald."

So my alias hadn't worked. "You talked to her, huh?"

"She was over here today. Did you hear about her boyfriend?" I nodded, but she continued anyway. "He was killed last night, and I guess she didn't know where else to turn. It made me feel bad—what I said about him when you were here before."

"But your suspicions were right about him, Willetta."

She leaned forward in her chair, but only to grab her Whopper. She didn't seem surprised.

"He'd been in prison back in Illinois," I said.

She nodded. "I'm usually a pretty good judge of

character. Take you, for instance. I didn't think you were up to any harm. You have kind eyes.''

Kind eyes, huh? Flattering as that was, I couldn't quite look her in the face. Not until I confessed about the deception I'd tried to play on her.

"Okay," I said. "I'm really sorry for giving you a phony name. My real name's Mandy Dyer, and I was a friend of Thelma's.''

She cocked her head as if trying to place the name. "Oh," she said finally. "You're the girl from the cleaners who likes murder mysteries.''

I was pleased that Thelma had mentioned me to her next-door neighbor. Maybe that would give me a little more credibility when I told her the rest of the story.

Willetta was a good listener, although her eyes filled with tears as I laid out my suspicions about Thelma's death and the statement from Naomi and Frankie that Thelma went down into her basement all the time.

"I don't think Thelma did go downstairs," I said. "She told me she couldn't get up and down the steps anymore, and since her washer and dryer were in the basement, she asked me if I'd have our delivery service pick up her laundry when she needed it done.''

Willetta nodded. "I'd wondered about that, but like I told you, I convinced myself that us old folks sometimes do foolish things.''

Once I'd started, I kept going. "Anyway, I couldn't help wondering if Frankie had something to do with her death, and I started making inquiries about him. That's how I found out about his prison record. Did Naomi say anything about it?''

"She seemed bothered by Thelma's death this morning. She kept saying 'First Thelma and now Frankie,' as if their deaths were somehow connected. I asked her what she meant, and she ducked her head and started to cry."

I supposed Naomi could have meant that two of her close friends had died within a short time of each other, but I didn't think so.

Willetta settled any doubts I had. "Naomi finally said that Frankie hadn't wanted her to say anything to the cops about Thelma's never going down in her basement. He said they shouldn't get involved."

"I wonder if she knew about his police record."

"I don't know, but he convinced her that Thelma could have decided to try to get down there just to see what was in the basement. And I have to admit, that's what I thought myself."

I wondered about the significance of what Naomi had told Willetta. If Frankie were still alive, I would be sure he'd wanted Naomi to keep quiet because he was the one who'd killed Thelma. Could it really have been as simple as him wanting to keep a low profile because of his criminal record?

No, that wasn't logical. He'd either been in on the murder with someone else or he'd seen another person over at Thelma's the night she died and had been blackmailing that person. Why else would he be dead now? Could it even be that he and Naomi had done something to Thelma together, and when they found out she had no money, they'd had a falling-out and Naomi had killed her boyfriend? I was as confused as ever.

"When I was here before, you said Thelma had seemed nervous about something. I should have been honest with you then, but I'd already said I was from out of town so I didn't want to seem too interested in her.''

Boy, this was hard, although Willetta was making it a whole lot easier for me than it could have been. "Anyway, I wondered if you found out what she was nervous about.''

Willetta shook her head. "Not really, but when I talked to Naomi today, she said Thelma had been worried about someone.''

"Who? Do you remember?" It was my turn to lean forward in my seat.

"Oh, I remember fine. It was Naomi who couldn't recollect the name. Just that she was pretty sure it started with the letter *J*.''

I finally grabbed my Whopper before it got cold. "Do you know any of Thelma's acquaintances whose names start with *J*?''

Willetta followed my lead, unwrapped her Whopper, and struggled to open a packet of ketchup for the fries. "Not that I can think of.''

I took the packet from her, opened it, and handed it back to her.

"But now that you mention it," Willetta said, "I wonder if she was talking about the handyman who'd been over there for weeks sprucing up the place. I never did know his name.''

I remembered that the house had looked freshly painted when I'd come to remove the clothes from her basement for the clothing drive. "Was the handyman the one who painted the house?''

"Yes, and Thelma'd been surprised. The place didn't really need a new coat of paint. It had been the same color for years. But suddenly her landlord hired someone to paint it. Then the guy kept hanging around doing other things—trimming the trees and putting brand-new shutters on the house. Turns out the landlord was planning to sell it right out from under her nose.''

God, had I been completely off base with my suspicions? And how could I find out the name of the handyman and the owner, for that matter?

We sat in silence for a while, eating our Whoppers and fries and drinking the Cokes I'd brought. It was a relief to get the lie off my chest; Willetta was the angel, willing to forgive my transgressions.

I polished off the burger. ''Did you ever know that Thelma had a button collection?''

Willetta had just taken a bite. She nodded and waited until she swallowed. ''She told me about it once, but I never saw it. She said she had it hidden where no one would ever find it—''

She certainly did, if hiding it in plain sight on a bunch of dresses was really hidden.

''—especially the valuable one,'' Willetta continued.

Aha. So there was one that was worth more than the others.

''Did she say how valuable it was?''

Willetta considered the question for a while as she took little bites from the last of her French fries. ''I don't know as she did, but I do remember her saying that value is all in the eye of the beholder.''

''Do you remember if she said what the button looked like?''

''No, all I recall is her saying what I already told you—that it was all in the eye of the beholder.'' Willetta finished drinking the last of her Coke and then wiped her lips on a napkin.

I had one more thing to confess before I left. I cleared my throat and began. "I have to tell you something else. Frank Pankovich was murdered right outside my cleaners. I'm the one who found his body."

She looked surprised, but then the shock turned to sadness. "Oh, you poor child." She reached across the short space between us and patted my hand. "What was he doing there?"

I shook my head the way I had with the police and later with Mack and Travis. "I wish I knew." Then I launched into the confession about how I'd gone to Naomi's house the same night I'd come to her place, also under false pretenses. "I said I was looking for Thelma's nephew, but I don't see how anyone could have found out who I was from that."

"You poor child," Willetta said again. "It sounds like someone was trying to make it look like you killed him."

The remark didn't make me feel any better, but I guess I shouldn't have been surprised that she could see the obvious connection since she seemed to have a high degree of common sense. "Well, the girlfriend of Thelma's nephew knew who I was," I said.

"You mean the woman next door who looks like a raccoon?"

Obviously, Willetta was referring to Leilani's darkly rimmed eyes, courtesy of black eyeliner applied with a heavy hand.

"Yes," I said. "She brought me a bunch of old clothes Thelma wanted me to have for our clothing drive. They turned out to have the button collection sewn to them.''

Willetta smiled. ''Thelma was a sly one, wasn't she, if that's where she hid them?'' She turned serious immediately. ''You don't suppose Thelma's nephew and his girlfriend could have killed Thelma and then Frankie, do you?''

''I don't know.''

Willetta thought for a moment. ''They're heading home tonight, you know.''

That was bad news. I wondered if the police had talked to them yet. Or were they clearing out one step ahead of the law? Maybe I should call Detective Reilly. Then again, maybe I should just lay low. According to Travis, Deke had a business in L.A., and presumably the police could always find him there.

''The nephew—Deke, I think he said his name is— came over and introduced himself when he first got here,'' Willetta said. ''Then he came over this morning and told me good-bye. He said the rent's paid up through the end of the month, but they sold Thelma's car and got through clearing out the place early. He seemed like a nice enough sort—except for all that artwork on his body.''

That's not the way he'd looked to me, but that was from a distance and without Willetta's eagle-eyed judgment of character. Maybe I should rethink the nephew—or even go next door to talk to him. Somehow I couldn't bring myself to do it. Besides, talking to Willetta was one thing, but talking to Deke and Leilani was definitely something the police would not look favorably upon my doing.

I took the paper remains of our meal to the kitchen,

deposited them in a trash can, and rinsed off the dishes.

"I guess I better go now," I said when I returned to the living room. Even as I said it, I was reluctant to leave the presence of someone who seemed to have faith in me, even now that my wings had been clipped and my halo had disappeared.

"You take care of yourself, and I hope the police won't think you killed Frankie. If they do, I'll be one of those character witness for you." She smiled again. "I heard about them on one of those TV lawyer shows."

"Thanks, Willetta. I'll come back and see you sometime when this is all over."

I looked both ways before I went outside. The coast was clear, and I made a run for my car. Last time it had been dark when I left her house, but this time the sun had just begun its descent toward the mountains.

I didn't want to go home. I guess I was afraid the cops would show up for me at any time. So I went to City Park instead and found a bench that was still in the sun. This is what I'd yearned to do on Monday when Mack and I set out to visit the button club president. It was Friday now, and Monday seemed so long ago. So here I finally was in a park. But without a sketch pad and with no desire to draw. All I could do was think about the confusing information I'd learned today.

Thelma had been worried about someone whose name started with a *J.* I couldn't think of anyone connected with Thelma who fit the bill. But what if it had been the landlord or the handyman who'd been hanging around her place? Wait a minute. They couldn't possibly know my name. So how could they have known to kill Frankie outside the cleaners?

I watched the ducks and geese on City Park Lake. I took a walk to clear my head the way I'd wanted to do earlier in the day at police headquarters. It didn't help. I'd known it wouldn't. I kicked at the fallen leaves as I made my way around the lake, but I finally realized I was getting cold. The blouse and slacks I'd changed into to go to Willetta's were inadequate against the sudden drop in temperature.

I saw that clouds had moved in over the mountains while I was in the park. The whole sky had become overcast. It was like a metaphor for the way I felt. I didn't even know how long I'd been there, so I glanced at my watch. It was a quarter to seven. I needed to get home. I had an urge to lock myself inside my apartment and throw away the key.

With an attitude like that, maybe being falsely imprisoned wouldn't be so bad. Yeah, right.

By the time I got to my car and drove home, it was dark. A motorcycle was parked in one of the spaces near my building, and I panicked for a moment. What if Deke and Leilani had tracked me down? I checked it out and recognized Nat's Harley. It was better than a patrol car, but not much. I knew Nat would be waiting at the top of my stairs.

TWENTY-TWO

NAT DIDN'T EVEN let me get to the top of the third-floor landing.

"So what the hell's going on?" he asked when I was halfway up the flight of stairs.

That phrase again, and even though I'd been thinking of explaining the situation to him last night when I needed help, that wasn't good enough anymore. "I'm not going to tell you anything until you apologize."

"Okay, I'm sorry." He actually looked contrite, which was a novel expression for Nat. "I'm *really, really* sorry, and I apologize."

"All right, come on in." For some strange reason, I did my best thinking when I was brainstorming with Nat, and right now I was in desperate need of being thunderstruck by a brilliant idea.

I went to the refrigerator and tossed Nat a diet Pepsi. "This is the only thing I have. Take it or leave it." Then I got out a can of cat tuna and put a spoonful in Spot's dish. Even though I'd fed him earlier in the day, he always expected something when I came home. Talk about a spoiled feline.

Once that was accomplished, I popped the top on another diet Pepsi and joined Nat at the kitchen table, where my sometimes-friend had slouched down in a chair.

He gave me a weak smile. "I shouldn't have said all those things on your answering machine."

"Damn right, you shouldn't have."

"I've hit rock bottom, Man," he said, but by using his nickname for me, he wasn't scoring any points. "That's why I stopped by the other night when you were talking to Travis. Bunny dumped me."

I gathered he was talking about the Broncos cheerleader he'd told me about on his previous visit. I resisted the impulse to say I could have predicted it.

"So she dropped you for a football player?"

"No, that's the weird part. She gave me the heave-ho for a computer nerd who was setting up a Web site for her. He's only five-foot-five." Nat seemed completely devastated by the fact that he'd been jilted for someone even shorter than he is. "When are you and I ever going to find our soul mates, Man?"

I shrugged, but I guess Nat figured that meant I'd forgiven him.

He was silent for a few minutes, but then his journalistic training kicked in. He should be thankful for that. His job was the only thing that pulled him out of the doldrums about his many failed romances.

"So what's the scoop on Frankie Panky?" he said finally.

"If I remember correctly," I said, "you swore on the answering machine that anything I said to you would be off the record."

He nodded, but I could tell he was torn between finding out what was going on and having to keep it secret.

I needed more confirmation than a nod. "So do you promise that this will be off the record?"

"Yeah, I promise." He sounded as if the words pained him almost as much as being dumped.

"Okay," I said, "the main thing you need to know is that I didn't have a romantic interest in either Frankie or Travis."

"I'd begun to suspect that, but I went kind of nuts when I saw Travis."

"That's an understatement, and I might as well tell you that Travis is a private investigator. When you didn't turn up anything on Frankie, I went to his agency, but I didn't know who ran it until I got there."

Nat ducked his head as if he were ashamed. "I went back to the office and checked him out, but I still hated it that you were keeping me out of the loop."

"So now that we're both calm and collected," I said, even though I felt as jumpy as a Slinky toy on a downward spiral, "I'll start at the beginning, but don't interrupt until I'm through."

Fifteen minutes later, I'd laid out most of the story about my elderly customer, Thelma Chadwick, and how her death had been ruled an accident but I thought she'd been murdered.

I gave my reasons: (1) She'd told me she didn't go down into her basement anymore; (2) The neighbors, Naomi and her boyfriend, Frankie, had said she went down there all the time, which I didn't think was true; and (3) She'd given me a button collection with a mysterious message inside one of the buttons—"not in a buttonhole" and "key/rock."

"When I asked you to look back in the newspaper files for a Frank Pankovich, I knew you'd go off on a tangent if I told you the whole story," I said. "But you're the one who jumped to the conclusion that he was a new boyfriend I was checking out."

Nat nodded. "You didn't do anything to deny it, especially with that 'Frankie Panky' bit."

I ignored the silly inflection he gave to Frankie's name this time. "Travis found out he had a record, and I was sure he killed Thelma until he turned up dead behind the cleaners. I don't think he knew who I was, Nat."

"Well, someone sure did," Nat said.

I outlined the rest of my suspects—the nephew, Deke, and his girlfriend, Leilani, who were clearing out of Thelma's place tonight, and even the button collectors, Mitzi Porter and Genevieve Atwood.

"But maybe I'm way off base," I said. "Another neighbor told me that Naomi said Thelma had been worried about someone whose name started with the letter *J*."

"Well, what about that other neighbor?"

"No, I'm sure it isn't her. She can hardly get around in her own house." And, in fact, I refused to believe that Willetta could be a murderer.

Still, something was bothering me, and for a minute I wondered if I should consider her as a suspect. After all, she was the one who'd told me about the mysterious *J* person.

Then it hit me. Genevieve. The name sounded as if it started with a *J*, didn't it? Just like Jennifer. Maybe people even called her Jenny for short.

Oh, my God. Could it be that Thelma had been frightened of the country club button collector? After all, Thelma had gone to her button club meeting once and maybe told Genevieve something that would be a motive for murder. However, it didn't seem logical that out of all the button collectors in Denver I could have sought information from the very one who'd been responsible for Thelma's death. That was too coincidental for even me to swallow.

I realized Nat had been saying something, but I'd missed it while I wrestled with my own internal argument.

"Aren't you listening?" Nat asked.

"Sorry. What did you say?"

"I was wondering about the note she left. Maybe there's a valuable button someplace on the dresses, and the key is that it doesn't have a buttonhole with it."

I'd already told Nat that I'd turned the buttons over to the police, but I'd also explained that before I did two people of rather questionable reputation had checked on the buttons and didn't think they were valuable.

"Besides," I said, "the note said the key to the puzzle was a rock. Mack and I thought maybe the rock referred to a diamond or some other precious gem, but we have no idea where it is."

"I have it," Nat said, shooting up from his chair like a volcano in eruption. "You said she liked all sorts of word games and double meanings, right? Well, what if she hid a diamond under a real rock someplace?"

I looked at him as if he had a few loose rocks rattling around in his head, and then I had a sudden thought of my own. "You know, you may be right."

He seemed surprised that I was taking his idea seriously. "You think something might actually be under a rock? Did she have a rock garden in her backyard?"

"Not a real rock," I said, "but what if she hid something in one of those phony plastic rocks?"

Nat looked blank.

"You know the kind I mean, don't you? The ones where a person hides an extra set of keys in case he locks himself out of his house. It would have exactly the right amount of space inside to hold a diamond or some other kind of button."

I wasn't sure if Nat knew what I was talking about, but he was willing to take the idea a step further. "And didn't you say that the nephew and his girlfriend were leaving tonight? Let's go out there and look around."

I started shaking my head.

Nat was already on his feet. "See, it takes your old buddy to figure things out. You should have come to me a long time ago instead of going to that Travis."

"No," I said, but I had to admit the idea did have a certain appeal. And even if we found a button that was only valuable "in the eye of the beholder," I couldn't help feeling that it would be the answer to everything.

Besides, the house was empty and Thelma's rent was paid to the end of the month. Thelma would have wanted me to do this. Or maybe it was Nat's enthusiasm and the fact that I was in such deep trouble already that finally made up my mind. How much worse could it get?

WE HAD THE USUAL argument about whether to take my car or his Harley. Nat pointed out that my Hyundai had already been seen in Thelma's neighborhood, but I hated to ride shotgun on the bike. I said I wanted to take my car so that I could carry my heavy shoulder bag and the flashlight we'd need to search for a plastic rock in her backyard.

At my suggestion, it was finally agreed that Nat would drive by Thelma's house on the Harley to survey the scene, or in this case, the term might be to case the joint. I would drive to the next street due east, park, and wait for him.

"The coast is clear," Nat said when he arrived at our designated meeting place. "The house next door where you said this Naomi woman lives is dark, too."

I'd changed into burglar black, a dress code Betty had once advised for breaking and entering; Nat was in jeans and his black leather motorcycle jacket. I personally thought our attire would make us look like Deke and his biker babe to the untrained eye. Never mind that Nat was about half Deke's size.

Act as if you belong here, I kept telling myself as we walked around the corner to Thelma's block. Her house might be dark, but its new coat of white paint seemed to send off a reflected glow like some sort of aura. It made me uneasy, but since Naomi's house was also dark, this was probably the best opportunity we were going to have.

I shuddered as Nat and I crept into Thelma's backyard, sneaking up the driveway between the houses as if we were up to no good. The weather had turned cold, and the wind had kicked up, sending dry leaves swirling across the yard.

When we got to the back door, I opened my shoulder bag and pulled out the flashlight. My eyes swept across the yard and the houses on either side. There were no lights, even in the back of Naomi's house. Willetta's house was also dark except for a flickering light coming from behind the drawn shade in her living room window. She must be watching TV.

Nothing moved along the back fence that separated Thelma's yard from the one in the next block. Fortunately, it was one of those high wooden fences that had become a running gag on the old *Home Improvement* TV show where no one ever saw the neighbor's face. Thelma's fence shielded us from the lights of the homes behind us.

I bent down, turned on the flashlight, and sent its beam across the ground by the back door. There was a scattering of rocks to either side.

"Hold this," I said to Nat, handing him the flashlight and motioning for him to lean down beside me.

"What exactly are we looking for?" he asked, hiding the light with his body as best he could.

I frowned at him, although I don't suppose he could see me in the dark. "I already told you. It looks like any other small rock except it's plastic and has a hiding place inside for a key. My mom used to have one outside her house here in Denver."

I picked up several rocks, but I could tell by the texture that they were only rocks. I tossed them back onto the ground.

"Hold the light steady, will you?" I wondered if the wavering light was a hint that Nat was as nervous as I was.

Finally, my hand touched a rock that seemed

smooth and not as heavy as the others. I jumped to my feet, losing the light altogether.

"Up here," I said. "I think I found it."

Nat popped to his feet, more agilely than I had done. I always maintained that he was double-jointed.

We huddled together as I carefully slipped the top open on the pretend rock. It was easier than it had been to open the locket button. Nat beamed the light inside.

My excitement turned to disappointment.

"It's a key," Nat said, as surprised as I was.

So Thelma had fooled me once again. The key to the button mystery wasn't a diamond or even a clue inside a rock. It was just what it sounded like—a damned key to her house.

TWENTY-THREE

"THIS IS JUST LIKE a scavenger hunt," Nat said, recovering a lot faster than I had. "Okay, let's go inside." He sounded as if finding the key gave us carte blanche to enter the house.

"No, we can't do that." Snooping around the backyard was one thing. Breaking and entering—even just entering—was quite another.

"Why not? It's obvious that she wanted us to do this."

That had been my rationalization before, but now I stated a much more obvious fact. "She's dead, Nat."

"Yeah, but you said the rent was paid until the end of the month."

Nat had always been a bad influence on me, or at least that's what my mother had claimed. Even though I felt an uneasy quivering in the pit of my stomach, I made up my mind. After all, we'd come this far.

"Okay, turn off the light." I scooped the key out of the phony rock, and shoved it toward the door. "I have a feeling I'm going to regret this, but as long as we're here..."

I dropped the rock back on the ground and felt for the keyhole in the door. I used my finger to guide the key into the slit. If I wasn't meant to do this, I was sure the key wouldn't fit or else I'd never be able to get it in the keyhole with my shaking fingers. Yeah, right, Mandy, you're living in a dream world of rationalization.

The key turned, and I heard the tumblers fall inside the lock mechanism. Nat twisted the doorknob, and we entered the house. Too late to back out now. He turned on the flashlight so we could see when we were in the kitchen.

The table where Thelma and I had shared a pot of tea on my one and only other visit was gone. I remembered how the room had been bright and cheerful, its walls painted a canary yellow. There'd been a rocking chair near the table, and Thelma had said she spent most of her time back here because the living room had always seemed like a dark, gloomy place.

The rocking chair was gone now, too. The place felt lonely as well as empty, devoid of all vestiges of Thelma. Somehow it strengthened my resolve to find out what had happened to her.

Nat plunged on into the living room. The flashlight darted across the walls as he shined it around the room. Like the kitchen, the living room was bare. To my relief, heavy drapes were drawn across the windows.

"I guess we're too late," Nat said. "Everything's gone."

"Give me the flashlight." Even though the place was empty, I was whispering.

"Why? It's a lost cause."

"Just give it to me."

For once, Nat obeyed.

I played the light across the walls again. Thelma had been right about it being dark in here. The beam of light seemed to be swallowed up by the walls. It was because they were knotty pine. I remembered them from my other visit.

"Okay, let's go," Nat said. He always had a short attention span when he lost interest in a project. Either that or he was having a delayed nervous reaction.

"Not yet." A strong feeling of déjà vu came over me, but it wasn't about the house. It was about my visit to Mack's rehearsal of *To Kill a Mockingbird* the other night.

Weird. I put the flashlight down to my side as I tried to think what was bothering me. It had something to do with the man backstage who'd been whittling a doll out of a bar of soap.

"There's no need to hang around," Nat said. "If there was anything here, it's gone now."

Darn, I'd almost had it, but it had slipped away. "Just give me a minute, okay?"

The thought was just beyond my reach, like a name I was on the verge of remembering. I needed to concentrate. I turned off the flashlight; maybe the darkness would help me focus enough to reach out and grab the memory.

"Hey, what're you doing?" Don't tell me Nat was afraid of the dark. Maybe I'd discovered a hidden weakness of his.

"It'll only be a second."

The man at the theater had been making a soap doll for the play. He'd said Boo Radley, the strange man who lived across the street in the play, was supposed to have made it as a gift and hidden it for Scout and her brother, Jem, in an old oak tree.

"Look, I'm leaving," Nat said. "Are you coming or not?"

Not. Knot. The man at the theater had said Boo hid his gift "in the hollow knothole" of the tree.

"I have it." My voice rose with excitement and seemed to bounce between the walls of the empty room. I turned on the flashlight, throwing the beam up to the walls with their knotty pine paneling. "I think Thelma hid something in one of the walls."

"You're nuts," Nat said.

"No, remember how she wrote 'not in a button-hole'? It was one of her little plays on words. She could have meant that it was hidden in a knothole in here."

Nat mulled my statement over for a second. "You know, that sounds completely off-the-wall, but you may be on to something."

My excitement was making me giddy. I laughed, although I don't know if Nat was even aware of what he'd said. I fought to regain control of my emotions. "You have to help me look for a loose knot in the paneling."

"With just a flashlight?" Nat asked. "It'll take all night."

I went over by the front door, flipped a switch, and turned on the overhead light. "Is this better?"

"You really are nuts," he said. "What if someone sees the light?"

"Better a steady light behind the curtains than a flickering one that would really make people suspicious."

I guess Nat bought the idea. He went over to the wall by the door and began to run his hands across the wood surface. Half an hour later, we hadn't found anything but solid walls with decorative knotty pine burls in them.

"I don't think she'd hide something way up high where she couldn't reach it," he said, wiping his dusty hands on his jeans as he glanced up toward the ceiling, "so I guess that's it."

"I was so sure we were going to find something." I was disappointed, but I wasn't about to give up yet. I took the flashlight and walked into the hallway that led to two bedrooms. Both were empty, but one must have been intended as a den. It, too, had knotty pine paneling.

"Come here, Nat."

I was already inside the room when a phone started beeping. The sound scared me. I jumped, losing my grip on the flashlight. It clattered across the floor. I'd been keeping my fear under control, but suddenly I felt as if my whole nervous system had been short-circuited. I reached down and retrieved the flashlight, ready to make a run for it.

When I got to the living room, Nat was standing in the middle of the floor talking on his cell phone.

"Jeez," I said. "Will you turn that damned thing off?"

He frowned at me as he listened to someone on the other end of the line. "Okay, I'll be there in twenty minutes." He punched a button to break the connection and, I hoped, turn off the ringer.

"What do you mean—you'll be there in twenty minutes?" I asked. "You can't leave now."

"Duty calls. There's been a big pileup on I-70 just north of here and they need me to cover it."

By "they," I assumed he meant his city editor. I wondered if that's why Nat had insisted on bringing his own transportation. He saw himself on call twenty-four hours a day, which might account for why he had trouble with relationships. I can't count the number of times he'd told me how he'd abandoned a girlfriend in the middle of a date to go ambulance chasing somewhere in the city.

"But I found some more knotty-pine walls in one of the bedrooms," I said.

"Give it up, Mandy. We aren't going to find anything. Now let's get out of here." He started for the back door.

"No," I said. "Go on. I'm staying here." If I'd been one of his dates, our relationship would have been over now. As it was, our friendship might very well be over, too. After all, he was the one who'd had the bright idea to come inside, and now he was deserting me. "Just lock the door on your way out."

"Okay. I'll stop by your place later to see if you found a hidden treasure," he said with a touch of sarcasm.

I was so furious with him that I didn't even answer.

The back door closed behind him, and I was alone. A few minutes later, I heard the roar of his motorcycle as he revved it up on the next block. Damn him, anyway. My anger fueled my resolve to prove I was right. I went back to rubbing my hands over the walls of the den, looking for that elusive loose knot in the wood paneling.

As time passed without my finding anything, my optimism faded. Maybe knots in knotty pine never loosened. My nervousness returned. Nat had been smart to leave. I should have gone with him. An inner voice told me to go right now, but I argued with myself. It would only take a few more minutes to check the whole room.

I'd turned off the light in the living room, suddenly afraid that a neighbor might decide to check up on the house, the way I'd feared someone was doing when the phone rang. I was relying on the beam from the flashlight, which I was holding awkwardly under my arm or in my mouth, to continue my search. Outside the wind was still blowing, and I jumped at every slight creak of the old house as I touched the walls.

Somewhere in the distance I heard the noise of a souped-up car on one of the main streets. It was coming this way. Or could it be Nat's motorcycle? Hope returned. Maybe he'd had second thoughts about leaving me alone and was coming back to rescue me. Well, maybe not rescue me the way Travis had thought he was doing that long-ago day of my bicycle accident, but at least help me so that we could leave together.

The motorcycle turned the corner onto the street outside Thelma's house. It sounded as if it was pulling into her driveway. Nat shouldn't have done that. He should have parked over on the next block, the way he'd done before, but maybe this would be okay. Neighbors would simply think it was Deke and Biker Babe returning to the house.

But what if Nat was in too much of a hurry to be cautious? Could he have seen the police in the neighborhood and decided to come back and warn me? I stopped what I was doing and turned off the flashlight.

I heard footsteps, then a voice at the back door. It didn't sound like Nat, even though he'd been known to talk to himself. Worse yet, the back door opened. Nat didn't have the key. I did.

"Is it my fault I forgot your damned sleeping bag?" a man said in a loud, deep voice. "You were in such a damned rush to get out of here."

It had to be Deke Wolfe of the tattooed body parts, talking to his girlfriend. I panicked. I was trapped in the bedroom. I did the only thing I could think of to do. I grabbed my shoulder bag, put the flashlight inside, slipped into an empty closet, and shut the door.

I started to slide down to the floor, but I caught a thread of my black sweatshirt on a sliver of wood. Once I untangled myself, I eased down the rest of the way, landing on something soft and round.

It was rolled up in the corner of the closet. It felt suspiciously like a sleeping bag.

TWENTY-FOUR

DEKE AND LEILANI sounded as if they were standing in the middle of the kitchen screaming at each other.

"If you hadn't goofed around all day," Leilani yelled, "we wouldn't have had to pack up in such a damned hurry that you forgot the sleeping bag."

"So where the hell is it?"

"It's in that closet in the back bedroom."

I eased open the closet door, scooted the sleeping bag into the room, and pulled the door shut again. I wasn't worried about their hearing the door if they hadn't already heard my heart, which felt as if it were about to blast out of my chest.

Surely when they discovered the bag out in plain sight they'd become suspicious. I scooted down into a fetal position, wishing there was a knothole in the floor large enough for me to disappear into.

Deke and Leilani were still arguing. One of them, probably Deke, was banging on something in the kitchen. Even that didn't override the pounding in my chest. If Deke had murdered his aunt and Frankie next door, he'd be sure to kill me if he found me here.

"We could have been up in Black Hawk playing the slots by now," Leilani said. "You promised me a good time if I came along on this stinkin' trip."

"That's when I thought we'd be stinkin' rich."

Maybe he would confess to killing his aunt for the hoped-for fortune that didn't materialize. No such luck.

"Now we won't have time to get up there and play before they close," Leilani whined. "Whoever heard of a gamblin' town that rolls up the streets at night?"

What time was it? Ten maybe. They had time. I wanted to shout out that the casinos in Colorado stayed open until two in the morning.

"We can still get up there, poopsie," Deke said, apparently having a change of heart. "Where'd you say the sleeping bag is?"

"I'll get it myself." I heard footsteps coming in my direction, and I scrunched into an even tighter ball and held my breath. As if that would help if Leilani opened the closet door. The light came on in the room. "You stupid jerk. It isn't in the closet. It's here on the floor. You must have been blind not to see it."

The appearance of the rolled-up sleeping bag beside the closet door apparently hadn't set off any alarms. Leilani retreated to the kitchen—with the sleeping bag in hand, I hoped—and I let out a whoosh of pent-up air. To my ears, it sounded like steam coming out of a locomotive, and I trembled for fear Leilani might have heard it, too. She left the light on in the room; I could see it through the crack under the door, and I was afraid that meant she was coming back.

There was more grumbling, and then I heard Deke again. "Hey, look, babe, I'm sorry." He sounded as if he was nuzzling her neck. "Let's just stay here to-night. We'll get an early start tomorrow, and then we can spend all day up there."

"Cut that out," Leilani said. "You know I get crazy when you start blowin' in my ear."

Oh, God, no, this couldn't be happening.

"Let's just spread out the sleeping bag in the living room, and I'll make Momma real happy." I felt nauseous anyway. Their sweet talk made me want to throw up.

"Mmmmm," Leilani said. Apparently, it didn't have the same effect on her. This was definitely not a good sign.

I had to figure out a way to get them out of the house so I could engineer my escape. Either that or make a run for it when they got naked. Better the first option.

Slowly I pulled myself to a sitting position, lifted the flashlight out of my shoulder bag, and dragged out my new cell phone. I turned on the flashlight and punched in the numbers for Nat's cell phone. An operator said the party was not available. This was a hell of a time for him to turn off the blasted phone. Of course, I'd been the one who'd told him to shut it off, but when had he ever listened to me before?

I ran through my list of co-conspirators. It was a woefully short list. Mack was at his final dress rehearsal, so he was incommunicado. Stan Foster would obviously be a bad choice. The only other person I could think of was Travis Kincaid, but desperate times called for desperate measures.

What was his home number? He'd given it to me, and I'd slipped the card into my bag. I felt around in my bag until I finally found it.

I punched in the number on the back of the card. A recording told me the phone had been disconnected.

Unfortunately, things seemed to have connected in the living room. I could hear groaning.

My nerves were frayed. Maybe I'd misdialed. I looked at the card and punched in the number again. The line was busy. A recording said that for seventy-five cents the phone company would call me when it was free.

Oh, God, he was probably talking to a girlfriend and would be on the phone for hours. I tried again as the gyrations continued in the living room.

The phone rang three times. A man finally answered.

"Is this Travis Kincaid?" I whispered.

"Sorry, what'd you say? We must have a bad connection."

I repeated his name, this time trying to enunciate more clearly but without raising my voice.

"Yes," he said, so apparently he heard me. "Who is this?"

"It's Mandy Dyer." Jeez, was this humiliating. If it hadn't been for my fear, I would have hung up. "Look, I'm hiding in a closet at—" At least I remembered Thelma's address. I gave it to him. "Did you get that?"

"Yes, but I don't believe it."

"The people who've been staying here came back, and I need you to come out here and divert their attention"—I wasn't sure anything could do that at the moment—"so I can sneak out the back door without them seeing me."

More sounds of ecstasy from the front room. I hoped Travis couldn't hear the noise.

"Maybe you could come to the door and pretend to be a sales—"

"Don't worry," he said. "I'll figure something out. I'm on my way."

Leilani let out a squeal of delight before I could shut off the phone. The couple was probably so oblivious that I could have gotten out of the house right then without any help. Then again, it sounded as if it were a quickie. I heard more thrashing around, and then nothing.

As an afterthought, I turned the phone to its vibrator mode. Maybe it was all that secondhand sex that made me think of it. No, I told myself, it was just a precaution in case Travis got lost and had to call me back for directions. Instead of putting the phone back in my purse, I stuck it under the waistband of my slacks.

"I'm hungry," Leilani said from the front room. "Let's go out and get something to eat."

Damn. Don't tell me they were leaving when I'd just humbled myself by calling Travis.

"How about that place downtown with the great ribs?" Deke said.

"Sure, babykins, anything you say. Zip me up, will you?"

Yep, they were definitely leaving.

A few minutes later, I heard the back door close and then the sound of the motorcycle as it pulled out of the driveway. By then, I was back on the cell phone, trying to head Travis off. What should I say to him? That it was all a joke? There was no answer, so I didn't have to figure out an excuse just yet. He was apparently on his way. Maybe I could simply leave town, never to be seen or heard from again.

Instead I got up, every limb stiff from being scrunched up like a pretzel on the floor. I'd been so tense that my body felt like one giant muscle with a cramp from head to toe. My left leg had gone to sleep. I leaned against the wall for support and tried to acclimate myself to being upright. When I pulled away, I snagged my sweatshirt on the same splinter that I had caught it on before.

I yanked myself away from the wall and opened the door. Leilani had never gotten around to turning off the bedroom light, and I debated whether to continue my search or get out of there before Travis arrived. I turned to shut the closet door, and as I did, I saw what had been snagging my sweatshirt. The closet was also finished in knotty pine, and one particularly big knot looked as if it were about to pop out of the wall.

No way could I leave now, much as I would have liked to avoid Travis.

I could see a depression under the knot where it appeared to have been pried out and then forced back into its hole. I began to dig at the swirl of wood. I broke a fingernail to match the one I'd broken when I tried to open the locket button two nights earlier.

I took it as a sign that I shouldn't give up. I used my thumb to dig at the knot of wood. I was sure I was finally on to something, even though the knot wouldn't budge.

Just then I heard a loud pounding, the kind Deke had been making in the kitchen. It shook me up even more than the ringing of Nat's telephone had earlier. Where was it coming from?

The banging continued, and I finally realized it was someone at the front door. If it was Travis, he was really fast. If it wasn't him, I might have to consider making a dash for the back door after all.

What if I didn't answer the door? Surely, the person would go away. But the banging got louder. Whoever it was, the person wasn't going away.

Finally I went to the front window, opened the curtain a crack, and peered out to the porch. It was Travis, and I still hadn't figured out a face-saving reason for the panic call I'd just made to him.

To hell with it. I couldn't leave him standing out there for the whole neighborhood to see. I took off a chain at the top of the door, twisted a dead bolt, and yanked the door open. "Come in." I grabbed his arm and whisked him inside.

I guess he knew it was me. "I thought I was supposed to rescue you from the people who lived here," he said. "Mind telling me what this is all about?"

"Later," I said. "The people left, and I think I've just discovered something." I replaced the chain on the door, reset the dead bolt, and motioned him to follow me to the bedroom.

"And to think I always had you tagged as the prim and proper type," he said.

I ignored his remark and pointed inside the closet to what I'd been working on. "Do you have a knife? I think there's something behind that knot in the wall."

Travis reached into his pocket and extracted a knife with several blades on it. He opened the smallest blade and handed it to me.

I gave him an A-plus for not asking any questions right then. I wiggled the blade into a crack at the bottom of the knot and slowly worked it out of the wall.

There was a nail attached to the back with a string wound around it. Just be careful, I told myself, so you don't lose what's on the other end.

Despite Travis's presence, I couldn't contain my excitement. I'd been right about Thelma's game-playing message. At the end of the string was a little velvet bag. I eased it through the hole, opened the top, and emptied the contents into the palm of my hand. It was a single copper button with the initials G.W. in a fancy script on the front and other initials in smaller circles around it. I squinted to read the other lettering: "Long Live the President."

Of course. I'd seen the button before, but only in a photograph. Mitzi had shown it to me in a book and asked if Thelma'd had one like it. She'd said Genevieve of the country club set would give her eyeteeth for one of the buttons.

It was a George Washington inaugural button.

"George and Genevieve." I must have said the names aloud.

"What?" Travis asked.

"Nothing." But they both sounded as if they could start with a *J*. Maybe Genevieve had killed Thelma, despite the coincidence of my seeking her out from all the button collectors in Denver, or maybe Thelma had merely said she was worried about "George," the button she knew someone wanted.

"If that's what you came for," he said, "I'd suggest we get out of here."

He didn't know that Deke and Leilani had gone to downtown Denver for dinner and probably wouldn't be back for another hour, but he was right. We needed to leave. I closed the knife and handed it to him.

"Okay, I'm ready." I put the button back in its little velvet bag. I placed it and the knot it was still attached to in my purse, and moved into the hallway.

Too late. I heard a noise at the back door. I had to be imagining things. Then a key turned in the door just as it had before. I was almost to the living room, but I stopped.

The back door opened, and a beam of light from a flashlight stronger than mine zapped through the house like a laser beam. There was no escape. Not after I'd chained the front door shut and reset the dead bolt. Travis must have realized it, too. Before I knew what was happening, he grabbed me and yanked me into another closet. Only trouble was, this one was a closet in the hall that only two brooms could fit into comfortably.

My body pressed against his as he pulled me in after him.

"Shhh," he said, putting an arm around me to close the door.

I was in a state of panic, partly because I was jammed in a closet with Travis. The other part was because I was wondering what had tipped Deke and Leilani off that I was here. They must have snuck back without the motorcycle to see what was going on, and this time they probably wouldn't stop until they found us.

The only thing good about being squeezed in a closet the size of a very small phone booth was that at least we weren't in the one in the bedroom that had once held the sleeping bag. Leilani could have realized something was weird about finding the sleeping bag outside the closet door. If she'd come back to check out that closet, it would be empty, and maybe they'd leave again. In your dreams.

Travis put his other arm around me, holding me so tightly that I was sure I would have felt a shoulder holster if he'd had one. Damn. Why didn't he have a gun?

I'd been a fool not to get out of the house when I had a chance, and now I'd involved someone else in my stupid scheme. Someone who wasn't taking this whole thing seriously. The situation didn't get any better when my phone started vibrating at my waist. It was even worse when Travis noticed it, too.

"What are you trying to do—turn me on?" he whispered in my ear.

"I really don't think we should be doing this," a woman said, which echoed my thoughts exactly.

She sounded as if she was right outside the closet door, and she definitely wasn't Leilani. "But if you think there's something here that will solve my Frankie's murder, I guess we have to try it."

It was Naomi, but who was with her?

That person apparently turned on the living room light. "I know you always said it was dark in here," Naomi continued, "but it's really spooky now that there isn't any furniture."

And suddenly I knew who it was: the person who'd said Thelma lived in a dark old house. But the outside of Thelma's house was white, and as Willetta had told me just this afternoon, it had been the same color even before it had been painted a few months ago. The only reason Naomi's companion would have described the house as dark was if she'd been inside and lied to me about it.

"There's something in the basement I want to show you," the woman with the little-girl voice said. "Come on over here, Naomi, and we'll go downstairs."

At that moment, I was sure Mitzi had killed Thelma and Frankie. I didn't know what part Naomi had played in the murders, but I had the awful feeling that Mitzi was planning to kill her, too.

TWENTY-FIVE

"I DON'T WANT to go downstairs," Naomi said. "Ever since Thelma died, I've been having nightmares about it."

"Oh, come on," Mitzi said. "The thing I want to show you is in the basement."

"No." Naomi must have stepped from the living room into the hallway. She bumped against the door of our hiding place.

"I said come on." Mitzi was in the hall now, too.

"It was bad enough seeing poor Thelma through the basement window. Please, Mitzi, don't make me go down there."

"Then you shouldn't have let your skinny little boyfriend mess with me. Now get going." Mitzi's little-girl voice was filled with hate.

From the scuffling noises, it sounded as if she had grabbed Naomi and was trying to drag her out of the hall.

Naomi whimpered in pain. "What are you talking about? What are you going to do to me?"

I couldn't stand by and let this happen. I reached back and grabbed the doorknob with my hand as I pulled away from Travis. He put his arms around me more tightly in an effort to keep me inside. Of course, he didn't know what I knew, so he must have decided I had lost my mind.

"Let me go," I said in a loud whisper.

The noises outside stopped. "What was that?" Mitzi asked.

"I didn't hear anything." Naomi was crying. "Please, stop it, Mitzi. You're scaring me." The sound of scuffling resumed.

I broke Travis's hold on me and almost fell out of the closet. Mitzi let go of Naomi and tried to look around to see what was behind her. Before she could, I lunged and tackled her at the knees of her purple pants suit. She hit the floor facedown. It was like a giant redwood crashing in the forest.

A sharp pain went through my shoulder and kept going up to my brain. I tried to ignore it as I held on to her legs. I knew I was no match for the heavyset button collector, but I was trusting that Travis would provide back up.

"Oh, my knee," she groaned, as she tried to crawl away.

"Don't look around." I clambered up and straddled her back. "I have a knife."

Call it wishful thinking. What I had was the flashlight. I'd given the knife back to Travis, but actually its tiny blade was suitable only for prying knots out of walls and peeling apples.

"What the hell?" Mitzi reared up like a bucking horse.

I whacked her with the flashlight, but I only hit her shoulder. She was going to throw me any second.

I did the only thing I could think of to stop her. "I